Of all Things, Great and Small

By

Jordan G. Farrell

And so, the journey begins...

Contents

Prologue

I lose no ground to you for I am the ground on which you walk.

I lose no pride to you for I am the greatest glory of them all.

I lose no life to you for I am the soul of all people for which they pray

I lose no battle to you for I am the conflict for which it is fought.

I lose no prize to you for I am the best of all things great and small.

I lose no logic to you for I am the only next step to take.

I lose no time to you for I am the clock by which it is kept.

I lose no souls to you for I am the place where all souls reside.

I lose myself to you for I am the one who vanquishes the "me"

to understand the "you."

~

A jet passing overhead woke the traveler in his bed. He sweat profusely such that the heat of his body reeked of the bacteria living on his skin, enjoying a feast of lipids and salts spewing forth from his overheated flesh. The virus within his bloodstream enjoyed chewing on his respiratory system and gratifying itself in an orgy of reproductive free-reign. He couldn't sleep. He got up out of his sweat-soaked flannel sheets, smelled his body odor permeate his nostrils, and compelled himself to write in the dim photons of the clock and cell phone indicator light so he could feel not so quite alone.

December 12, 2034. 2:17am.

I dream of not dreaming, the way most people do. In my dreams, I do mundane things–horribly mind-numbing, meaningless, menial, mundane things–things that dissuade anyone else from living–really living. They suck the soul from my consciousness and bury it in the wasteland of anonymity. The places I go, and the creatures I seem to be, throughout any given day is nothing more than a perception, a phantom, a glean in our Lord's eye. How is it then that anyone else forcing themselves into these dreams, continue to have the same dream, day in and day out? Is it just their way of denying that they are alive? Is it their way of bleeding their souls, so that only the husk remains? I dare not fathom.

The dream I have is that I am a human being, with a mate and a home. I do menial things to maintain this home and perform boring, useless tasks that create nothing and serve only to repeat again later. Like I said before, the curse of the mundane! I would wake (in my dream) at the same time every day, travel to the same location, and interact with the same people. I would drive myself insane by not knowing anything about the world, life, the cosmos, and especially, how to perform correctly for the people I was with. How am I supposed to perform? I would spend every "waking" moment trying to figure it out.

I feel very anxious all the time (*anxiety!*) in my dream because others were so bent on giving their opinion—and ignoring mine. They would talk much but say little. It was a strange dream, indeed. I would become physically exhausted after only sitting all day. I would be bored out of my mind and have no outlet for anything worthwhile, like the secrets of the cosmos, or creation. I cried out screaming many times in my dream. You know, I think I am going to call it a *nightmare*.

I love to reflect on this recurring nightmare that has entrapped me. Every time I go to sleep, I think that things there will be different, better. Alas! I am deluding myself into thinking so, for the forces in this nightmare are stronger than any one man's will alone. Basic assumptions of existence that you and I take for granted do not exist. It is a crime in my dream world to assume. It is a crime in my dream world to expect the use of common sense. It is a crime in my dream world to be better than anyone else. And it is a crime in my dream world to even state your opinion! All because this thing called the "state" removes necessary life forces (*freedom!*) from you for doing so—your home, your mate, your life. I awake screaming each time I enter back into my reality, the unique and visual place of my heart I thank God for every single day, the places of my true self, my reality, and my life.

They are the places unique to me, and common to everyone, really. Everyone: They are those, whose lives are exact, irreversibly constant, but forever variable. It is for you, stuck in your nightmares like mine, probably difficult to accept a thing that is both a variable and a constant. But, that is the true nature of the cosmos, is it not? Truly, the whole point of quantum mechanics is that everything exists in probabilities, not constants. So macro-mechanics must work that way too, right? It is the *only* way really. Some probabilities are more constant than others are. However, there are always exceptions to every rule—*every* rule. How we perceive these variables is directly related to the way we perceive the reality around us. This relativity of experience is the force of universal consciousness. The relative variability of an event is directly proportional to the psychology of the observer. The memory of the observer's events is the container that holds the cosmos for that observer. Many observers are many containers of events. When observers communicate to each other, they create common frames of reference we happen to call *the cosmos.* The cosmos exists because of the thought that creates it. It cannot be defined any other way. That is what the Lord does, as is His will of the creative force that is His power. Since He created us in His image, we too possess this power.

Somebody in one of my dreams said, "Nothing is but what it is made to be by the alchemy of the system." I guess that means if no one was around to tell me that something is yellow, I cannot know what *yellow* is, because there is no system of description (*no communication*!) to guide me. Then, left to our own devices, we then know not of *yellow* and what it means. Yet, yellow as a color objectively exists, as a specific wavelength of light we perceive as yellow. Thus, yellow is both a particle of finite objectivity and a wave of perceptive variability, which is the very definition of quantum mechanics and the principle illustrated by Schrödinger's cat.

We know what hurts and what feels good, but pain and pleasure are facts of existence. We know when we can see, and when we cannot, because sight and blindness are facts of existence. We know when it is cold, and when it is not (and hot and when it's not), because relative temperature as a function of thermodynamics is a fact of physics. We know when we are hungry, because we objectively require nourishment to survive. We know *not* of time and its passage, but we are told of it based on our memories. Thus, can we know what we know without being told we know it? Or does knowledge exist as an objective fact and we thus experience it in different ways based on our experience, and level of sentience in that experience?

We know when we are thirsty, but we know not of water. But we do know that the vast thing over there with the clear substance in it makes our thirst go away when we suck it in through our mouths. If no one is telling us—raising us—to know such things, *as* things, we are nothing but observers of events. We imagine what to do based on what we are taught to do by others. If we don't copy successful behavior in others to survive we die. That's a fact.

But we also dream. We fantasize. We have imagination, and in that imagination each of us can envision an infinite number of worlds—cosmoses—in which to exist. And since the very definition of "cosmos" is "the encompassment of all things," then everything we imagine must exist in the cosmos because it fits within the overreaching definition that is the infinity of all things. The alchemy of our imagination is everything, in everything. Our perception is the building block of the very cosmos itself. Conversely, if there is no observer, no imagination, then there is no cosmos to observe for me. But I live in many cosmoses in reality, each and every night, through the lives of all creatures, great and small.

The places in which I exist—not of a nightmare—I perceive are wonderful places where I learn all about the great truths of the cosmos. They are nothing like the recurring nightmare I experience every day that is my waking existence. I am compelled to share them with you, to help you; to help all who wish to experience reality in many forms, who have a splinter in their minds about what can be real. To help you refill your husk of existence, the pedantic dribble of daily events that the dream (*nightmare!*) dictates to you as *reality*. No one can say you are wrong, and no *thing* can take your cosmos away—unless you don't exist. Since we all exist, we all exist.

I open this journey to you now. Keep reading this journal. Be patient. Be introspect and in a quiet place and the wonders of infinite possibilities will open for you...

But now I must sleep (*or wake! What's the difference, really?*). I need to work in the morning (*evening!*), is my guess.

I

Perseverance

I lose no ground to you for I am the ground on which you walk.

December 13, 2034. 3:33am.

I woke in a chilled, damp place that the tunnel of light that transitioned me from my nightmare to where it leads me to all the time. It is the same as it always happens, and this time I arrived in a cold, sunless morning, just before the dawn. I had fallen from my night-place on the side of the tree and landed on the cold, wet grass below. I could see my breath as I exhaled through pours on the sides of my thorax, and my wings were waterlogged and heavy as I struggled to right myself.

"Today is my birthday," I thought to myself, staring up at the tree. Its sides were smooth, as it was a young tree. The leaves were not yet out fully, as the light times were still shorter than the dark times. I needed to walk up there to catch the first rays of warmth of the light time. Oh, how I loved it so! The relief, the lightness, the joy in my heart as the heat permeates my body! Yes, today is my birthday—the fourteenth time of light. My first showing of light was fourteen times ago, and in fourteen more times, my time will end. Now every day is my birthday.

"I feel so heavy, and I have to get up this tree." I said with an infinite sense of purpose behind it. I started up its side. My feet's ability to adhere was compromised by the added weight of the water in my wings. As a result, it was like carrying the weight of ten heavy rocks on my back. Such is the burden of my life I suppose. At the base of the trunk, it's not so bad, but as soon as I made vertical, the weight was overwhelmingly noticeable. "One—foot—at—a—time." A heavy breath, and then a rest. At least I could see where I was going. Sometimes I would end up the wrong way and have to back it up the tree to my place on the limb. That *does* take a while!

Once I get a rhythm going though, I manage to do alright, as long as I don't meet any obstacles. I think that obstacles are put in our way to show us that we are not invincible, like God telling us that we should just be what we are and not be everything to everyone. Some of us get more obstacles than others. I suppose that those others are a little more thickheaded than I am. Sometimes I see others of my kind meet many obstacles, many ferocious obstacles. I saw another attacked by red fire ants on their way up the tree, and the poor devil, he did not make it past. Shame of it. Oh well. I need to get up this tree.

"Hey you! Hey you down there! Hurry up! The light's coming!" Someone shouted from their limbs above me. It must be nice not needing to worry about everything, as I do. It must be nice to be completely oblivious. They obviously don't remember *their* nightmare like I do. Of course, they taunt me like this every morning, like they have it so rich that they could never, ever be in this situation. They will be down here soon enough, and I will be on my limb, or another limb in another tree, whatever, and their arrogance will be reciprocated. Then the Day of Judgment will be for theirs!

"Juuuustin! You better get up here or we're going to throw things at you!" I looked up and there, a crowd began to form. The others started to wake on their own in anticipation of the upcoming light. This always happens to me. The taunting, the teasing, the dodging. Then one of the girls yelled down, "Hey, Justin! If you make it up here, you can have me all light long!"

"Yeah, whatever." I thought to myself. "I had you yesterlight all light as well. So did all the others on the limb. You laid your eggs and now you're empty again. No big motivation there, sister!" And with that I hunkered down and continued to climb and awaited the onslaught of debris from above. I looked up and beyond the crowd of butterflies above me and I could see the light at the very top of the tree. The race had started.

One. Foot. At. A. Time. That's all it takes. The rest will follow. The rain of sticks, twigs, and leaves started its course to me. I could hear the laughter of my cousins who caused me this discomfort as I struggled to avoid the bigger pieces. I thought that perhaps the worst thing that could happen was that I would be knocked down to the grass again and I would have to start over. And in reality, that fact was true. But to them, *to them*, this was "kill or be killed." They were doing this to see if I could survive. The scary part for me was that I would be up there doing the same thing if the roles were reversed. Whatever, I need to get up this tree.

It stopped. I was still inching forward. They had run out of stuff to throw at me, or they simply got bored with my lack of terror. Maybe that will deter them from doing it next light. It was quiet again. I stopped for a moment to catch my breath and took in the cool air. Ah. Life is good, I am good, and soon I will be basking in the warmth of the light. I looked around and it was getting brighter indeed. However, I looked up at the top of the tree again and I could see that it had moved down the leaves to almost half way to my limb. I was yet to be halfway up the trunk! I needed to hurry!

Now that it was peaceful around here, I could concentrate on my climbing. I made good progress for a while and was almost to the mid-branch when I spotted it. A web, directly blocking my path to the top. It was gracefully made so that one side was supported by the mid-branch and the other supported by the trunk, forming a canopy of grayish-white transparency almost all the way around the trunk. I couldn't tell if it was all the way around because my angle of perception blocked the lea side of the tree from my view. If you thought climbing up a tree with waterlogged wings was hard, try moving from side-to-side around on the circumference of a smooth trunk with waterlogged wings! It's not happening! There was no way of avoiding this obstacle, and the light was making its way relentlessly down the top of the tree.

"I wonder if the spider who made the web is still there." I asked myself. I couldn't tell from the perspective. All I saw was the silk, and no movement. No husks either. That was promising. Maybe the spider who built it a few lights ago abandoned it due to the fact *we* were too smart for her and she couldn't get a meal. Maybe she's dead already, and all that's left is the remains of the egg sack that was once full of baby spiders but is now empty because they all left to find their own homes. Hmm. Maybe I was going to walk into it and get stuck, and have my guts sucked out of my body like milkshake by a young and voracious arachnid who is just starting out in life! I think maybe that I will go up there and see if I can get around the thing, without disturbing anybody who's home. I need to stop dwelling on the negative, because that will surely get me killed this light. Speaking of which, the light was relentlessly coming forth and I had yet to get past the middle of the trunk.

Onwards and upwards. So, here I am staring at the bottom of this death trap, trying to figure out if there's a way around this thing without getting caught. I was feeling a little lighter as my wings were starting to dry out. They weren't as waterlogged as they were when I first got started, and I was thankful for that. So, I decided to chance falling off and go to the side—the *side!*—and see what was available on the lea side of the trunk. The problem though is that once I was there, the wetness of the lea side would make it quite slippery. The lack of exposure to light at this time of the day kept the dew moist. I had to be careful. One step at a time and everything else will follow.

So, there I stepped, nice and slow, around to the left of the trunk. My wings, although lighter, were not nearly dry enough to carry my body weight in flight. So, if I fell, there I would be, back in the dew-soaked grass having to start all over again. I was not too worried though. I was sure I would be careful enough to make it all the way around.

As I peered around and looked up at the web, I could see that it was not connected on the lea side. There was a way to get up past the web without disturbing it and consequently being successful at preventing me alerting the spider-devil-predator. I was encouraged to the point of excitement! Then I got careless. I thought that once I was past the gap in the web there would be clear sailing until I got to my limb. I could get there well ahead of the light and take a short nap before it comes. Damn, I'm good!

Then, what's this? I'm stuck. Am I stuck? I *am* stuck! Damn! One of my feet was caught in some sap that had run down the side of the tree. Damn! This is *not* good. Now I can't move *anywhere*! I'm going to have to struggle quite a bit to get out of this. I must get out of this. I am right next to the web. If I even touch the web it will disturb the spider, and then she'll come to me, wrap me in the cocoon of death, and carry me to the web. All this avoidance will be in vain! I must be careful, but forceful.

I leaned back, as it was the only way to avoid the web altogether, and flapped, and flapped, and flapped, as hard and as fast as I could to get out of the sap. I did not—I could not touch the web. Slowly, I could feel my foot slipping out of its entrapment. Slowly, slowly, a little looser. I was getting tired. If I couldn't get free soon I would not have any strength left in me to continue. I would exhaust myself to the point where I would just die, hanging on the side of this tree by one foot, staring at the grass below. I sighed. Then I was free.

Falling to the grass below, I landed with a bounce on the soft blades. It was dark, but strangely, not wet. Wait! This wasn't grass I was on. What was this? It was like grass, but finer, and I was moving up towards the top of the tree. What could this thing be that I was on? I had no idea. It was enormous, and warm. Very warm! Maybe my wings could dry off here. Then suddenly I was going upward, higher and higher. I was resting but moving up without moving. It was miraculous to me. Never before had I experienced the sensation of moving while being still! It was a transcendental experience!

I realized that if I could jump at just the right moment, I could land myself on the side of the trunk of the tree twice as high as I was when I was at the spider's web. Now I just have to get up and make it through the thicket of fine hair to the surface towards the front of this creature I was on. It was a tough walk, but it wasn't anything I couldn't handle, since I wasn't as water logged as I was before. Plus, the heat, emanating from the surface of this creature was drying my wings quickly. I reached the summit until I could go no further on foot. Then the creature lunged towards the tree trunk again. I jumped, and landed exactly where I imagined I would be, almost three-fourths the way to my limb. I was almost home free.

I looked up at the top of the tree again. The light was lower than before, and before the time before that. I thought, "My God! I wonder if there will be any more obstacles like the one I just faced, bizarre as that was." I turned around and saw the beast from afar. It had two shiny spheres that followed my every move. An oblong, irregularly shaped container that had three openings encased them. Two of these were small openings, shiny and positioned next to each other, horizontally. Their placement was below and centered between the two shiny, following spheres. Below them was an opening, gaping, that had hot air coming out of it. With that hot air was a long, pink object that was coated with liquid and hung there out of the opening but exhibited some signs of independent movement. Behind this container were all the fine hairs that I was entrapped in. I could see no end of it from my position. Whatever, however, I must climb this tree.

I expected all the others to come back and taunt me more by this point as I took my one step at a time up the trunk. But, they had long since gotten bored with me and my antics. Too bad, no one was around to witness my feats of unbelievable skill! Well, I exaggerate, but it was a bit of good luck that got me this high, and I was no wetter for it! I got along fine for a while, one step at a time, and I expected to reach the limb soon.

I stopped for a minute to soak in the view. This high up the tree, the grass below seems like one large field of green, as from this distance one cannot discern individual blades. My wings felt good. They were feeling only damp by now, but as of yet, no powder could be coating them to allow me to fly up to the limb. There was not too much left to climb. The light on the top of the tree was very close. I should be there soon.

The limb came into sight. I gazed at it for a time and contemplated my final ascent over the top and turning, facing towards the light, soaking the golden heat of the rays, feeling the warmth, and just being. I would breathe slowly and contently as the core of my being was gently caressed by the glow of the sun. I would stretch my wings; out, in, out, in, and out again, letting those life-giving rays dry my tired, sore wings, lightening them at every beat. Then, when I was dry as the air around me, and as warm as the life the light gave me, I would jump off and take to the air! In flight, I am me! In flight, I see all the land and all the water around me! In flight, I feel the pull, across the great sea, with the sun always at my left in the morning and my right in the evening. The fulfillment of what I have become. From worm, to husk, to me, I am free! I will find a new mate, on a new land, in a new tree, on a new limb, and fulfill my purpose—

to *be* what I am, to be what *I* am. My soul ached and yearned for that moment. I climbed, assured that that moment was here, in very short order.

I was almost there, just a few more steps. Turn, Justin, turn! The limb was beneath me and I perched myself on its smooth bark. I looked up towards the light coming down to meet me. I was filled with anticipation. All of the hard work and challenges that met me to get to this point were now going to be rewarded, made their worth by the ends of the journey. I stood, breathless at that moment as I perched high on my legs. I closed my eyes and waited for it to come. I stretched my wings as wide as they could go, waiting for it to come. I waited. I waited. I waited.

Finally, it came. The glorious warmth of the mid-springtime sun quenched my heat-thirsty body. My wings stretched on bent on their own, as if by their own accord. The happiness I had felt knowing I would be rewarded for all of my effort, now became the fruition and culmination of all of the pain, anguish and suffering I volunteered my body through. I paid for this place in my life, and now I was being repaid for it with my reward that is my new station. The cosmos was my good and dear friend, for the cosmos always repays you for all of your deeds and efforts, *and* failings. Everything we do, everything we say, it can be said, that is to be said, must be said, back and around again to you.

My wings thoroughly dried in the warm sunlight after a few minutes, and with that final thought, I took to the air to find the life that the cosmos had provided me in justice.

II

Hum

I lose no pride to you for I am the greatest glory of them all.

December 14, 2034. 4:34am.

In the between, I saw a haze of flapping wings, fur, and light. I was sleeping, and I inevitably fell back to the nightmare that plagues my existence in this world (*awake!*). I was aware that I was in great need of acknowledgement, of purpose, and of purposefulness from others; relying on the noise of others for my own validation, which made me ill. I was the one too smart to be included, but not smart enough to be a master of anything. I was not masterful in any way! The obsession always got in the way. The need for it, the obsession embrangled my soul into something other than it was meant to do. I found myself focusing slowly on the enemy within my nightmare who shows herself first as my friend and mentor. She calls herself, "manager" as if to say I need to be managed. She is, indeed, the soul who manages to torment me every day. She does so well to deconstruct me—the one who, if she would just let me be who I am—whom the cosmos' Creator made in its image—would forever be rewarded and not punished for her faith in me.

Faith. That is indeed an *odd* concept. Faith, it seems, is where one has full belief in something with little or no supporting evidence to substantiate that belief. But that evidence, any evidence in a practical sense within my nightmare, is so often ignored by the tormentor. Thus, it is difficult for her to have any faith in me—I fail, it seems, to have any credibility in her mind even with mountains of evidence behind my words. Upon my attempts to show her the evidence, she does not believe, and does not trust, or she simply refuses to see it. It is grossly ironic that so little faith is placed in a fellow human being, and yet time and time again, she demonstrates infinite faith in the benevolent Creator who provides little physical evidence of His existence. It is an exercise in frustration I do not care to maintain for long.

I certainly am losing respect for the tormentor as a kindred spirit as time marches along against her. The tide will soon turn in my favor for the battle of supremacy over all others who oppose me, or those who simply appeared to me to be breathless. A metaphor? Indeed. But the breathless ones with no soul give me cause to crush them and devour their spirits with all of the power and glory that the cosmos' Creator had given me as part of my existence here, like a Lion. The nightmare is becoming a thing to look forward to, and to embellish in, at least this time.

~

A bright lighted tunnel, and then I wake! I found myself trapped within a cell of wax. I felt heavy with moisture that tasted sweet to my senses as I ingested it. I could not tell what I was doing in this place or what my purpose was, until after some time had passed when the urge to escape from the prison I was in was too strong to ignore any longer. I pushed my body against the top of the cell as I noticed all around, for the first time, all the while there was a constant hum—a sound that never diminished or wavered—a tone, a tonic, music to my ears, of one harmonious chord that told me I was home.

After a bit of a struggle, I found myself surrounded by others of my kind, but different in the slightest sense, who were very eager to help me escape from my prison. Across the vast combed surface of the plain, I saw that others of that kind were helping another of my kin in the same manner as I was helped. I knew that I would never be able to ignore that fact until—until, well, I guess the show will go on until it stops.

From all around me, as I struggle through a vast crowd of others, all began cheering, “All hail our new queen! All hail! Hail! Hail!” I was taken aback by that but realized quickly that I was certainly different, if not superior to all the others around me. I was bigger and stronger than those around me—and from what I was...*before*. I was the best of everything in *this* world, and my instincts told me it was all true, as a true Queen.

From across the combs however, me, and those immediately around me, heard the same cries to hail the new Queen. In panic however, I realized the cries were not for me, but for another. My instincts were very strong, and very sure. I wanted no part of sharing my kingdom with another of my kind. I felt the desire—the wanton need—to challenge and kill her. It was a bloodlust that overwhelmed every fiber of my being and I could think or feel of nothing else. All those around me and all those around the other began to merge, and I approached the other swiftly, as she approached me at the same rate.

“You are not to be Queen!” I yelled out through crowd, and the hum all around me. “I am to be the Queen, the best of all things, for all to obey and serve!”

From the other side of the combs, but getting closer, “You are not to be Queen! I am to be Queen, the best of all things, for all to obey and serve!” Jostled by the fact that the words coming from me were instinctively being said by my challenger also, I slowed my pace toward the impending battle. I stopped and thought for some time about what was happening. Surely, I could not be saying these things from something I learned from somewhere else at some time. I was just—just *born*—and had no idea about sentient behavior at all. I was, as was she, acting on pure instinct—genetically transferred memories and knowledge that allowed my species to survive and to flourish, as we all knew we must. I was not in control of my actions, what I said, or how I felt. I was being led by an unseen force—a force within my genetic code to go and defeat the rival to my supremacy as quickly and as decisively as I possibly could. This was not me. *This* was history being made from history already made.

She called out to me once again, "You shall be destroyed, and I shall be victorious! You shall perish and your challenge to my authority will fail!"

I retorted with exactly the same words, "You shall be destroyed, and I shall be victorious! You shall perish and your challenge to my authority will fail!" It was instinct. I was not doing the calling, my body was. There was separation from what I was doing and what I thought should be done. I was not in control. It was like I was under the influence of a powerful stimulant that created the power and desire within me to kill, like a puppet with strings attached to my very soul.

Our relative positions decreased incrementally as each step we took towards each other closed the gap between us. All the while the crowd of others grew more and more excited—awaiting the final closing step that would be the beginning of the challenge for the right to be their Queen. I was ready. She was ready. And so, it began.

Not anyone could be prepared for the pain of the first blow—a needling, stinging pain, that slowly took the energy out of me. I had no choice but to do the same and I jammed by smoothed ovipositor into my opponent—death to *her*! I poked and thrust my stinger into my rival, to injure her—to kill *her—her*! Let there be hate, and let the war do the work it will! For, *war works*! The crowd all around was cheering in a grotesque display of survival and strength that I knew was the best, right path. Call that *genetic memory* as well. We grappled with each other as our legs and feelers were bent and moved with great force against their natural orientation. Pain had no definition any longer. It was all anger, and mechanism of survival (*—war!*), to breathe, to rule, as Queen. I was the best of all things, and I knew I would rule. And I knew that my perpetual mirror image of myself felt and knew *exactly the same thing* about herself. After all, we were all all-powerful clones.

The crowd pressed against us, thus avoiding the possibility of being trampling by others. It was a small but open space that was always kept secure (*sacred!*). The two of us would have the opportunity to be in a winner's circle or a circle of death, depending what became of the outcome of this battle. I cared not about what would happen after. I didn't know. I had faith that my destiny was laid out in front of me if I won this battle, whatever it was, and that it would unfold in its own good time. I had faith that that would be so. I had faith in the faith that I had, which made me stronger, and made me fight harder, over the pain, beyond the trauma, beyond the existence of the challenge—it was all for—for—...

"For the Hive!" I cried out as I thrust my sting into her thorax, up into and through her neck so that its end could be seen jutting through the other side of her body.

The silence was deafening over the hum of the crowd. And they were motionless for a brief period, as more powerful genetic memory clicked on for the next set of events.

"All hail our new Queen! All hail! Hail! Hail!" raised the crowd. Over and over did they sing my praises! Over and over did they pledge their loyalty! The challenger remained motionless, as I peered over her husking, draining corpse. Others in the Hive began to move her—carrying her like the waste of mammalian filth—slowly, but consistently, over and out of the Hive, down to the ground, to meet her final demise.

I basked in the glory that was my new-found power over the one who had opposed me. The Workers had no choice but to now follow their genetic memory, their instinct, me, and now to collect pollen for the Hive. The rush and exuberance of the moments during the battle were over. I was then escorted to the chamber where Queens lay claim to their throne and fulfilled their destiny. The Queen's Chamber was the room in the Hive where I was at the seat of my power, and waited on, feeler and foot. The next thing that my body was telling me to do was breed. Build the Hive! Build the Hive! There was, however, no Drones to breed with.

One of the Workers came to me and said, "The Drones will be ready in a couple of suns, your majesty."

"Excellent!" I responded. "I have little patience for my duties."

"Yes, your majesty."

"What is your name, girl?"

"I am Jessica, your majesty."

"And you are a Worker here for how long?"

"Oh, suns and suns, your majesty! I have served the Hive for many, many suns! And I will serve you with the same vigor and excitement, if you will allow me the honor, your majesty."

This wasn't verbal communication, like mammalian filth, mind you, but a more finessed, refined method of body language, signs, and hums. All the symbolic gestures and noises that created our language were highly complex and evolved. But, as of yet, we as a species were not quite ready for sentience. I was not, certainly. Let my genes lead the way! Oh! How simple life would be from now on! Oh! The sweet taste of victory! Oh! The sweet ignorance of non-existence perceived only in the moment!

A few suns had passed, and the time had come for the releasing of the Drones (–the *suitors!)*, the life-blood of the Hive. We only made them to use their genes. They served no other purpose. Males themselves serve no other purpose in the Hive. Men are weak, useless. They build nothing. They exist only to serve me, their Queen! Their role here is finite and certain. Sentience would destroy that–the Drones' role, the Workers' role, my role–all is predetermined by what previous generations did before. Our survival ensured that their legacy would endure, and our species would survive. That order would be destroyed by sentience, and sentience in all cases creates chaos, because with sentience comes agenda, and the need to control. And with agenda comes conflict, and with conflict comes destruction.

All species–save one–fight for two reasons and two reasons only: superiority and food, in that order, both of which are never or rarely deadly. I say rarely, because obviously in my species the battle for supremacy is always deadly–for the loser. As Queen, however, I was not allowed to see such things, or even to remember such things. I existed only in the instant of time that I was awake and aware. For me, and my kind, there is no past, no present, and no future. All was in a moment, an instant, absent of forethought, logic, and all reason. All is emotion and instinct, as the animals (and other insects)! Sentience would bring awareness and would destroy the Hive. All that we have achieved in our species' survival over the eons would end. But again, as Queen, I was not allowed to see such things.

The Drones came in one by one, in single file, approaching me slowly. They were neither revered nor ignored by the Workers, but they were merely *tolerated.* They were tolerated for the very short time that they would be in our—*my*—midst, and then, they would be thrown away like mammalian filth. Many Drones visited my chamber in the next suns, and I bred with them. So many there were, I would not remember as Queen, but I knew there were enough to repopulate the Hive for another season. That is, they provided the raw material I needed to create the population that would replace all of us in the next season.

As each one was finished with their life's work, a group of my best Workers, Jessica and others, took them, overwhelmed them and discarded them out the entrance of the Hive. There was no fanfare, no respect, and no sense of glory in the act. Males are garage! Use them as they should be used! It was a necessary function of the Hive to survive, and the Drones existed only for that purpose. Upon its completion of impregnating me, my subjects I own, there was no longer a purpose for them to serve, as the slaves to my glory that they were.

And I spent the rest of my days fulfilling my purpose. I laid egg after egg, and my Workers would carry them off and deposit them into newly minted cells—the cell from which I came—and fed them the sweet nectar that I was covered with upon my immergence.

I lost no pride to the Hive for I have been the greatest glory of them all. Thousands of eggs meant thousands of new Workers for the next season. I have fulfilled my role for the Hive and the Hive would survive yet another season. But as the air became colder outside, I felt my worth diminishing—my strength, draining, my usefulness, dying. My purpose was almost fulfilled. The genetic memories of my ancestors running out, until the point where there was no longer any purpose for me. Hibernation was upon the Hive. The time for eggs and breeding was over, and I felt the force that kept me awake and aware of the actions of my ancestors slip away. And then there was a spark of thought in me that said, "You too are the slave, as the males, being discarded after your usefulness is worn out. You are a slave to the Hive. And now you're no longer useful, and you must die." I shook in terror as my energy waned on.

The hum I had around me for so many suns that I had taken for granted, and let slip from my mind, suddenly was very loud and forefront on my mind. The security of the hum of the Hive was there, and I became dependent on it for *my* peace of mind. The hum that abandoned me as soon as it was clear that I was useless. The hum, then, at the end, became less pronounced; the hum was fading into the distance, slowly, and became just a dim mist in the ear of a Queen whose time (whose genetic sexual script) had run out, her purpose fulfilled, her beliefs and all her thoughts and dreams forgotten, except for the genetic memory I had passed to my children, and it became suddenly, darker, and it was all very, *very* quiet.

Darkness. Terror. Oblivion.

But again, as Queen—as *Bee!*—I was not allowed to see such things, and I forgot them, in the infinitesimal moment that I was.

III

Projection

I lose no life to you for I am the soul of all people for which they pray.

December 15, 2034. 1:55am.

The nightmare returned, worse than before, not knowing whether I would care or not, or whether I would ever wake from its horrible terror at all or not kept me in a profound state of panic. It was so hopeful that it had finally assumed a created place in my mind that allowed me to control it—so to look forward to its arrival. But, alas! No. The nightmare didn't care about my feelings. I knew it didn't know it cared—the nightmare—at least I knew it didn't and it knew that I didn't know. To know is to know nothing except what I projected.

This time I saw the unleashing of hell coming from the skies, riding upon peaceful vehicles of shiny metal and great power. Their creators were peaceful and loving of all creatures great and small. But, this day their users were the devil incarnate. Any other day their users sought only life, liberty, and the pursuit of happiness, and freedom. They allowed this for all who wished it, for all others who cared, and for all others that needed a chance at a new life. "A new life," what a novel concept! We all know we only have one this time around.

There was the great city of these peaceful, but vain people, who sought nothing but their own desires—be they great, small, pure, or perverse, but they were their own grand end to so many who prospered in a place where prosperity was the end upon itself. They wished to be left alone but sought to show others to do the same who perhaps did not wish to be shown. Be that as it may, they in no way deserved the hell unleashed upon them in the nightmare of my own perception.

I saw two towers made to look strong and mighty. They were the symbol of all that was great about the greatest civilization the world had ever known. And the people in their shadows feared of nothing, as citizenry of that great nation in a complacency never was achieved prior in all human history. It existed for all the worthless, the homeless, the rejects, the poor and forgotten of all the other nations of the world and was the strongest because of them, and it was also the weakest because of them. As open as she was, she was most vulnerable because of them. Her greatest strength turned out to be her greatest weakness.

Innocence is a strange thing. The act of experience diminishes innocence and can never be regained. But experience is something that can never be lost and must be gained to thrive. One is indirectly proportional to the other. And *that* is what is called *life*. So, I guess death is sometime when there is no more innocence–it runs out–and all that there is in the soul is only experience, like some grand fraction where the numerator (experience) is a part of the denominator (innocence), and when the numerator equals zero, therein lies the end of life, because anything divided by zero does not exist. Blessed are the innocent!

There was fire. Great fire. The hate of the rest of the world in an instant all focused on the symbols of capitalism's success and socialism's abysmal failure. And it rained the flaming, burning, parts of people onto the lingering, stunned survivors. People faced with burning to death at 2001 degrees or jumping 2001 feet to a concrete oblivion chose the latter if they could. Who knows how many had no choice at all? They fell. The towers fell. The hearts fell. The spirits fell. The nation, however, strengthened, solidified, and united more strongly than ever before. Now to the world, "war" meant "justice," "retribution," and "revenge." Before it only meant senseless death. Never again did it mean that, because, war works!

Before, I had no worries about the future. Before, I had no doubt about a cure for my nightmare. Before, there was no way the trials of the world would affect me. Before, there were two towers where there is now only tragedy. Before, planes in the air where just something that were there. Before, I could not fathom destruction or despair. Before, this was a place of security and peace. Before, this was a place of multiple beliefs living harmoniously together without the judgments of micro-tribes and emotionally inept, delusional idiots complaining of their perceived oppressions. Before, this terror was something that happened to somebody else. Before, there was no way to distinguish one's self. Before, I complained it was too cold or of rain. Before, my heart was filled with disdain. Before, my life was directed and secure. Before, I could imagine the thought of forever, for sure. Before, we were innocent, naïve, and alive, but now, we are forever in fear, of what falls from the skies, and what comes out of mouths.

After, is yet to come. The response, the equal and opposite reaction, the constant of the cosmos–actions and reciprocal reactions– there is no escaping them. They will happen. The projection of evil and hate is reciprocated by the cosmos, in one way or another, with the same towards the doer of the deeds of the same. By the same token, however, the projection of good, caring and love will always also be reciprocated by that same cosmos, maybe. It doesn't seem that way sometimes, certainly. But truly, the cosmos, a mirror of our lives, is the truth and only truth. This nightmare was the worse one yet, and I suspect will be the worst one for a long while. Who knows. I also thought the last nightmare was getting better as well.

I stood, looking into the sun and my mind started to wander. The dream, the nightmare was ending, or beginning, and in the middle—whichever didn't matter—whatever, it didn't matter. Nothing did, anyhow. The sun, the tunnel, both were ever brighter in my mind, began stirring a notion of calm, of new life, of new existence. Suddenly the hellfire from the sky that was my nightmare was mercifully paused, suddenly.

Out into the light, I came, warm and blinding. To wit, never before experienced this time around. I fell onto a solid surface of rough, pointy things and a breeze chilled my wet body. A large creature, I knew that was of my kind, was licking me warmly, gently, easily. I smelled her—the imprinting—forever to be my mother, the giver of life and peace. Her golden face and warm, soulful breaths drawn in, told me she was happy to see me, to be near me, to love me. She licked me until I was clean, then a rumbling in my stomach told me it was time to suckle.

At that moment it was clear to me that there were others of my kind also suckling—siblings, I guess—I felt safe in their presence. Walking came naturally, as I moved around to get to her breast. These are the days of pure peace, of knowing of no evil, of pure goodness, of pure innocence. The protection I felt of the vast unknown around me overflowed around my need to explore, for a while, anyway.

As the days and weeks passed, I became the one to go out into the world, test new ground and lead my sisters and brothers to new locations, but never ever too far from all the mothers. I grew quickly to realize that a community of adults of my kind were forever joined—as family and would work together to feed us all. I grew older, and hungrier, and not for mother's milk, but for meat.

Mother would return to us and give us food from her mouth, something that wasn't in the least bit repulsive, but beautiful and caring. She gave me love (*food I didn't need to hunt myself!*) and I soaked it in, again and again, with no regard for future or time. After mealtime we all just lollygagged around, soaking in the rays of the afternoon sun, sleeping, cuddled next to each other. Sometimes, we'd end up under a shady tree, with the vast, open plain stretched out before us. It was getting warmer, and something inside was changing in me. It was an anxiousness that I sensed from all the other mothers. Everyone was getting edgy.

"What's wrong with everyone?" I asked my mother as she licked my back.

She said, "The males will soon come and fight for leadership of the pride, Justin."

"So?" I asked.

"So, it is the most important time of the year. It is the time where the strength of the pride is tested. It is the time of great change, new life, great pain, and great shame."

I did not understand. How could I have? I was new to this world and understood little of it. All I knew up until this point in my life was peace, joy, and contentment. The events of the next few weeks would be the watershed of my life—to change it inexorably. For the better? Perhaps. Perhaps not. It would turn out to unravel the peace and serenity that was all I knew until then. All the mothers were frankly unwilling or uncaring about my needs or the needs of any of my brethren, but for the basics in meat and water, did we follow them and were allowed to be as near to them as we wished. Things were changing. I was a good six moons old now and it was time, soon, to break out on my own. Soon, but not quite yet. It was something I felt but fought with my roaring insides against. My roaring insides. They kept getting louder after each rising of the sun. I was rising; I was rising into being, and I kept the cub in me quieter and quieter. Not of my own accord mind you, but just as a matter of circumstance—and of evolution. The fight within myself was between the safety and peace of being completely cared for by the mothers (*food without having to hunt it myself!*), and the safety and peace of being the most powerful male in the pride—the Father of my Pride. That day will come, but far be it for me to predict when.

Right now, however, I am the son of the current father. I am but one son. The other sons and I always played the games of dominance. We did this for fun, for the bonding, for the ritual. The bonding part became less important over time, and the ritual became more important. Fun, well, it was fun as I was the victor of the games—I was mostly the winner, most of the time and the mothers took notice.

Then the sun rose on a new day of my life. I was to join the hunt with the mothers. The memories of what my mother said about the male leader returning weighed heavily on my mind, and the anxiety that it carried with it, created an alarming sense of urgency— "know how to survive, or the end is then near." Anxiety of survival; I would become accustomed to that before long.

We left about mid-morning, as the sun was approaching its zenith, to search for the great herd of wildebeest that traveled the plains. My mother told stories of such creatures—the food of my loins, and of lions. The sun was always at our backs, so as not to alert the weakened eyes of our prey. I knew that. I was never told, but I knew that in my deepest heart of hearts, as instinct. The sun made the tall grass a golden glow of streaming light the same color as my coat. I was the grass. I was invisible to all. To all, I was not there. And to all, I was the hunter, the bringer of death, the finisher of existence, and now I was to make the hunt the reality that my mother's loins of lion-hood had made me to be.

"I am the hunter, the bringer of death, the finisher of existence!" I said aloud. There was a rush and rustle of sound far off in the distance. In my mind I could smell all of them, ten thousand strong, all waiting for the one thing they feared most, their own death, as they stood grazing aimlessly with no purpose other than to reproduce themselves. Perpetually eating, perpetually breeding, and perpetually dying. Bison, cattle, wildebeest, governments, whatever you call them, it doesn't matter, were all parasites on an ecosystem whose purpose it was, was to make food for other food at the expense of still more food. Any creature that serves no purpose than only to feed another, serves no purpose other than that of the other, as a resource for the other. Creatures that create the circumstances by which they survive, will survive and dominate all other creatures. Those who produce rule those who do not. I found that this is the universal truth of all things. For me, there was no other, for we were food for no one.

The mothers were all ahead of me, and I found that fact reassuring, albeit a little bit demeaning. I was, after all only six moons old, and I was sure no one expected of me what they would expect of an adult. I just loved to watch the mothers go in the grass and ever so delicately, creep upon the herd, that knew nothing of their impending doom—at least for one that day.

Wildebeest aren't very smart, you know. They kind of just look around and do nothing except eat, which I've stated. But they are *especially* dumb. I think if you had twenty-five wildebeest in a room and one dog, the dog could figure a way to get to some food left in a box, far better than a wildebeest. I don't know. That's just me talking. One thing they have going for them though, they have *solidarity*. No matter what, they stick together. They protect their young and each other. They stay together, through thick and thin, through the best and worst of times. They stick together, like lemmings over a cliff to their collective demise. Of course, after six seconds, they forget all those things.

"I am the hunter, the bringer of death, the finisher of existence!" I said inside myself, again.

So much food, so little time. The mothers gradually were getting closer to the herd. Soon it would be time to choose a target. The weakest one of what they can see; a young one or an old one, or a sick one it shall be. I personally prefer the young ones. Their meat is much easier to chew, as it is so very tender. Ok, I will stop drooling now.

I guess in a way I feel sorry for the bastards. I mean they don't really know what's going on from one minute to the next, with a two-second memory and all. So, they never learn from past experiences. All they do know is that when they smell, or see, or feel that there is a predator around the area, to run away as fast as they can, in the moment they feel it. That's it. Simple life, isn't it? All the while we're the ones doing all the work around here making sure that the rest of the family is fed and kept safe. From what I have no idea. After all, we *are* Lords of the Jungle, aren't we? That's what they tell me anyway. I hear the tiger clan's been talking some smack about they are being the lords. I think not. They're always so nosey, and certainly cannot run as fast as us lions! Yet, they like swimming....

"I am the hunter, the bringer of death, the finisher of existence!"

The time for the attack was fast approaching. The mothers were all signaling each other, as they always do, with their facial gestures and body movements. I copy them to make sure I learn the language. My mother was on the right flank, and I could tell by the direction of the others that a young bison was to be dinner tonight! The thought is very appealing, is it not? I stayed very low and very quiet. I risked nothing to endanger the hunt. I was to observe and that was all. I was not to interfere in any way whatsoever, or mother would scold me something fierce or worse yet, I would get no supper! I believe that she would break down eventually and let me at a bone or two though.

Then it happened. The mothers all leapt forward, and the herd reacted. The small one they were after tried to stay close to its mother. However, got left behind as its mother blindly stumbled away in the instant of panicked experience for a space away from us grand finishers of existence. The kid was left apart from its mother, apart from its herd, and apart from its safety in numbers. The kill was fast, but merciful, for sour meat is no joy to eat. My siblings and I all watched the events unfold from a short distance away, waiting for our turn for the spoils of the kill, the prey for which we all pray stays with us, for the sake of the family, the pride, for lions.

The dust of the great plain rose from the scene of the deed, and from whence it came, the herd retreated to a safe distance, back to grazing and lumbering about as if nothing had happened. Ah! The bliss of ignorance in momentary existence! This all except for the mother of the kid that was now our dinner. I could see the confusion in her face of something missing that was once there, but suddenly was now gone. It was a smell of something, a presence that she thought was there, but was now not. It was a memory, something. Then it was nothing. Just like that she was back to grazing in the golden grass of the great African plain. And I had my dinner with my siblings after the mothers were done with their share. Does prey grieve? Probably not.

Suddenly, there was a great stir in the distance. The herd, startled once more, moved violently farther away from the dinner scene. In the distance I could see a large male lion, great in mane and stature, ready for his share of the spoils. He was an impressive specimen to behold. His mane was as large as any I have seen, and other males have not as large as he. He let out a great roar telling us that this was *his* territory. The mothers backed away and prepared for the springtime ritual. As there was no challenger to the male, Sherlock; he would have his harem this year once again. I don't know for sure though, but that's what they tell me. Being only six moons old is really a pain. Then I noticed Sherlock was limping.

Off in the distance I saw my older brother, who had a great mane of his own, who let out his own great roar. Castile was his name and was as big as Sherlock. It's amazing what a few more moons will do! Castile approached the scene with great purpose, with hot breath, and with heavy determination. There would be a challenge this day; and for myself and my siblings, we would no longer know innocence.

Their eyes caught each other from a distance and they began to approach. The sun, golden, and making golden all things around–the grass, the coats, the bugs, their eyes, and the dust. It was a golden dream in any nightmare that any young cub could not, or ever, get used to. They approached closer to one another, slowly, but determined. They said no words, as words, give any indication of anything anymore. Only actions spoke as the two squared off in the middle of a dusty plain, on a land so far from anything, that if there were no observers to the events about to unfold, they would never have happened.

As the battle began, there were great growls and groans from both contenders, as two prize-fighters as entertainment in an arena of power and glory, not like that of gladiators in the Coliseum in Rome. That's what they tell me anyway. To see such a spectacle of battle was to be in awe of the sheer powers waged against each other in that battle for supremacy. The two squared off. My siblings and I cowered in the grass, trying to be as invisible as possible.

The two grappled for what seemed to be an eternity, for all we could see through rise of dry, choking plain's dust were the pauses in the action, and wounds inflicted. Both had them, but none wavered. Both were strong, and fierce. Both were worthy to be the master of our dominion. In totality, both were and could have been leaders of the pride.

Then Sherlock began to buckle. Our master, our father, was folding. The limp we had noticed before was far more pronounced and Castile took full advantage of the injury, by attacking on that side exclusively. Castile was merciless, and Sherlock had no choice but to acknowledge his own defeat, to that of his eldest son, Castile.

"I am the hunter, the bringer of death, the finisher of existence!" Castile cried.

Sherlock, our father, was our father no more. And no more was he the future of the pride. No more. And I was the first to realize this fact before all the others of my age as I watched the once great Sherlock slowly limp away from the pride; the sun hitting his back, pressing against his hind toward the slowly darkening skies in the east that beckoned his soul to come forth for the final time. I never found out what became of my father and no one spoke of or had seen him again from that point forward.

Then, as fate would have it, our education of that day took a turn for the worse. Little known to most, but I had an idea of such a thing, Castile's first role as Lord of the pride, was more violent and deadly than the merciless display I had just witnessed. He ran towards us—my siblings and I—and one by one trampled and murdered each and every one of them before my own eyes. The fear I felt was like none other experience before, nor since. The blood and cries of dying words coming from the ones who I called "brother" and "sister" were being squelched one at a time in a tirade of murderous wrath. I ran.

I ran through the grass as fast as I could, west, towards the direction of the setting, golden sun, so that its glare would blind my pursuer. I ran as fast and as far as my little legs and oversized paws would carry me. I kept running until the darkness fell around me and I found a place to hide inside of a hollow log that appeared to have been there since the beginning of time. I cowered within its cooling, dampened with dew interior, and panted. It was getting cold. There were no mothers to warm me or feed me. I was on my own, alone, hungry and afraid. There would be no more meals for me that I did not hunt myself. My youthful moons were over.

I did not sleep that night. I did not hunt either. The next day the sun warmed the log to dry its interior once again. I was hungrier still, and now thirsty. I had to find water, but I was too afraid to move from my hiding place without knowing if Castile was awaiting my departure to finish his work. I learned one thing from that experience: Fear equals power. That is how lions do it. That is how governments do it, and that is how I will take my revenge for the murder of my siblings and the disappearance of my great father. Castile had taken all that was secure and innocent in my life up to that point and destroyed it in the matter of a few seconds of fear. That is great power. The fear of annihilation in any of its forms is the basis for all power.

I learned very quickly thereafter that field mice were an easy catch, and so I hunted at night for them, taking me great distances from the lands I once knew. I found new places where there was water—even in the dry season. The competition was fierce, and I did come across other lions, but never my birth pride, but never the mother whom I suckled, never any other sibling survivors, and certainly never Castile.

Soon I was hunting larger game on my own and scavenging on kills that had been left by other predators, even lions, whose ownership was taken over by dogs and hyenas. Vermin! I was large enough now that my mere approach was enough to rattle them off the remaining carcass. It was never as beautiful as the meat of a young wildebeest, but it kept me alive, growing, and strong.

I was growing a mane of my own.

One day I came upon another pride of lions in the shade of a tree in the mid-afternoon sun. There seemed to be no other males in the area, and my instinct to mate was very strong. I was in the apex of my need to be needed by others of my kind. I was strong. I was powerful. I must be made to prove my value and show someone—anyone—that I was a worthy lord of any pride. This particular pride I came upon was twelve in number, eight of which were mothers, and the rest young, not yet a full twelve moons old. The season's drought had been especially hard on this pride, as the great mother told me that their father had died and many of them were starving, and thirsty. I negotiated a settlement with the great mother for membership in their pride, in exchange for my knowledge of my secret water hole that I alone seemed to know of. Not even the elephants knew of this place due to its remote location. I lead the pride over land for many days to this place and lost two more cubs along the way. It was in a basin, down a steep embankment, which for those not of full strength was very treacherous. But the need for water and food was great, and within its waters were small creatures that even the smallest of cubs could manage to catch for a light meal. But we were reacting in the moment. That is not how to lead a truly great pride.

"Enough of those," I told the great mother, "and your children will be strong and live a long life."

She agreed, and gave me her name, the name of her mother, and her mother's mother. That name was Jessica, and from that moment forward we were primary mates. I had the others as much as any other Lord, but Jessica and I shared a bond that few that ever came before rarely had the pleasure of experiencing. We enjoyed great pleasure amongst each other, and amongst our children. We claimed the water hole and the surrounding fertile land as our own and protected all of us with our lives. Few creatures dared cross our path. Again, fear controlled all others—except for the elephants, we let them have safe passage once they discovered our place. Besides, who wants to argue with a walking boulder that can squash you in one step, anyway? But for the most part, all other creatures, great and small, dared not oppose us.

Throughout all this there was finally great peace in my life. I knew nothing of the horrors of my old pride, under the reign of Castile. The pure projection of evil he laid upon the mothers and the cubs was unknown to me. While he rarely murdered a cub of his own seed, he was not the warm, caring caretaker a good lord should be, at least in my opinion. For all I know, Castile's way was the only way, the way it has been for generations, and eons of lion families. For all I know I was the aberration and Castile was the norm. I, Justin, freak of nature, caregiver of the careless! I sometimes thought of myself that way. I sometimes thought that I never really did belong, that my life was meant to end on that golden plain, so many moons ago. My life, as fulfilled as it was at this point, had a purpose that was not yet complete. There was one great task that I had to endeavor to fulfill. This was the force that drove me to survive in the log, moons and moons ago, through dry and rainy season after season, and it drove me as I lived my life with my new-found pride.

The rainy season was upon us once again, much as it always had been. We took shelter under an overhang in the precipice that created the water hole, just as we always had before. The cool drops of moisture served as a plaything for the youngest of cubs, as they rustled about during the day, playing their games of seek and destroy, and struggling for dominance, even then. I reflected that even at that young age all lions struggled for dominance, projected a need to the cosmos to be the strongest, the most in control, the most powerful.

For whatever reason, however, this rainy season was heavier than most. Water poured down the sides of the precipice in torrents and waves, as the rain did not let up for days and days. Hunting was difficult at best, and we all were feeling the pangs of hunger within our gullet. This drove us to petty quarrels amongst ourselves, and even between Jessica and me. How I loved her so. So, we decided to hunt. We had to. It was not much of a choice. The cubs were old enough now to observe the hunt, just as I had watched my mothers. So, the pride, as we left the safety of the overhang in the precipice, started our way towards the great plain once again. It was a treacherous journey; one that I knew may be my last if I did not lead my family as a good lord should. I was at point, and then Jessica, then the other mothers, then their youngsters. That was the order of all things, always.

We walked along slowly, carefully, with torrents of water both in front and behind us. The sound of the rain against the exposed rocks and water in the watering hole was deafening. Communication was difficult. I wish I could say that it was not. I wish I could say that I knew everyone heard me say "Stop!" when I did. I wish I could say that.

The falling water approached us from and passed over me and down the line of lions that was my grand pride. For whatever reason, the force of the water that hit me was not strong enough to jar me from my stance and grip on the ledge I happened to be on. Unfortunately for the others—*Jessica!* —the water fell with great force, sweeping them all down the steep embankment that was the precipice and into the water hole below. They lay silent, peaceful, as I looked upon their golden bodies on the rocks, under the rocks, and in the reddened, flowing water. I was in shock. I was the lord of a dead pride. I was alone, again. I was no one.

I wandered (*again!*) for days in the plain, not caring about the falling bullets of rain piercing the scrapes of my skin—not caring about food, water, or anything. I was a failed lord. My pride was gone. And my *pride* was gone. I no longer served a purpose. I controlled nothing. I was lord of no one or any*thing*. I stopped wandering, sat, and waited to die. Of course, I had no idea what that really meant. I didn't realize it was my lack of purpose, my lack of motivation. I sat, staring at the rain falling, and the anger built up inside me.

"I am the hunter, the bringer of death, the finisher of existence!" Perhaps.

The next day—when I didn't die after all—I got up off my britches and thirsted for a kill. Wildebeest were on the move again, and the sun was out yet again. The heat on my face felt so good after the coldness of the rain the night before. I was hungry and angry, and I was going to take out my frustrations on my dinner for the day.

I stalked as my mothers had stalked. I sneaked as my mothers had sneaked. I targeted as my mothers had targeted. And I killed as my mothers had killed. The tender taste of young wildebeest melted in my mouth like the warm rain water that I took the pleasure in drinking from. Again, I felt the power, the control, the immediate need to fulfill the last destiny of my life.

"I am the hunter, the bringer of death, the finisher of existence!" The savory meat smoothly went down my throat.

I knew that had to find my old pride.

I had learned a valuable lesson: those who seek peace and harmony will always fail because the unforeseen is more powerful than any one's will and powers of prediction. Sad as though that is, I knew what was projected upon me, my siblings and my pride long, long ago, must and will be avenged. I will reflect what this world has projected upon me. I will be the young lord who will challenge and defeat the former. I will murder *his* cubs, and I will take *his* pride-mothers as my own. I am lion, Lord of the pride! I am the hunter, the bringer of death, the finisher of existence! And I followed my long shadow away from the setting, golden sun, on a now flowering and awesomely beautiful plain that lay before me.

Several suns had come and gone, and in each one, I found no pride where once there may have been. Oddly familiar surroundings seemed somehow unfamiliar; objects were both smaller and larger—wider and longer. Was that the tree under which I suckled my mother so many eons ago? I quell the urge to answer. The thoughts were maddening. Was she still alive? Had she more cubs? Are they grown? Is one now Lord? Is there my pride? Is there my *pride*? Is it mine for the taking? Am I too late? I will—I *must*! —persevere. I will lose no life of my own either way. I am my life, what the cosmos is, what I am, are one and the same. I am who the cosmos has made me, the reflector of projection. I am me. Therefore, I exist!

Over the next rise I came upon a fresh kill of wildebeest, perhaps done within the last half-sun or so. The smell was ripe, but none too harsh. Insects had gathered with the vultures and dogs—I think I've said my peace about them. Off in the distance I saw them, at least some of them. They were mothers, freshly reddened by the blood and meat of their dinner. I did not know whether they were the mothers of my birth pride, but I longed for the membership and respect of others of my kind—Jessica! How I miss you so! —will there be another for me? Will I be accepted, or rejected out of hand? Do I dare ask? My mane is full and stout, I am a worthy opponent. I will prevail.

With that I approached. The mothers faced me and outright rejected me.

"Be gone!" One mother said. "You are not our Lord! You must not stay here. Be gone! Be *gone*!" The last 'gone' was lengthened by the growl of her rich and mature vocalization. I knew I was home.

"Wait!" I replied. "Are you not the mother of my life? Are you not the one I suckled as a cub? Is your name not the name of your mother, and your mother's mother? Are you not Rebecca, my birth mother, and now great mother? Are you not these things?" I paused. She paused and stepped forward, and we exchanged sniffs. She staggered back, as did I for just that moment.

"Justin? It cannot be! Justin?" Tears were in her eyes. "You are not alive! Castile murdered all of you, your siblings. But even then, here you are!" Her grayed golden coat flurried in the post twilight breeze that began to overtake the plain. The pink skies behind her created a warm pinking golden silhouette of her warm and friendly gaze upon her long-lost son. I was warmed by this, and the knowledge that the now great mother of my own pride had taken me in, back to the place I was once before.

"What of Castile, my mother? What of him?" I asked plainly.

"Tomorrow is another day my son. There is plenty of time enough for legends and stories on the new light of the sun. For now, let us share in our feast." I wish she told me that he was still alive. I wish I could have known that, but alas, therein lies the rub; one shall not know one's destiny before its own time.

We feasted for most of the evening, napping and lounging most of the time. The contentment of a newly filled gullet and the surroundings of family and friends was the stuff of contentment, like none that I had felt since the moons of the loss of my other pride. "Jessica, forgive me!" I exclaimed to myself under the influence of some insane form of guilt for being happy after her loss, and the others. "Forgive me for trying to start over." I explained to Rebecca about all the events surrounding my survival and the pride I took care of, and Jessica, and the other mothers; I told her of their demise, and my guilt. She licked my vast face and neck, and for a moment I was taken back to the days of my youth, the days of innocence and love, and laughter. I sighed and lumbered into a foggy nap. The next morning would be at another pace entirely.

Castile approached from the east, from the direction of the rising sun, following his long shadow as he came forth. The disenchantment in his stern look of a rival male with his great mother was as obvious as the great, long mane that surrounded his narrow mind. I knew not of his presence until the roar came from not a great distance away.

I startled awake, as did Rebecca. "Oh no." she whispered as she rose to interject her presence between his and mine. I rose, and all the force that drove me to this moment was suddenly gone. I could not summon the energy to confront the beast–the beast, Castile. I awakened further, however, and all that came before, the tragedy, the pain and anguish all became focused on the beast, Castile. I would be avenged this day, as would Sherlock, and all my siblings.

"Who dares bed with my pride?" he growled in my direction.

"I am me, Justin, son of Rebecca, son of the Great Sherlock, and rightful heir to my pride for which you have stolen and murdered! You have taken what is rightfully mine, and now I will teach you just in the reflection of your own, evil projection! For I am the hunter, the bringer of death, the finisher of existence!"

A great laugh came from Castile, showing is blatant overconfidence. I saw this and rushed him. I took him by surprise, a great advantage. He was strong—as was I. The struggle was fierce, and the dust of the battle enveloped the view for all others to see—just as in Sherlock's time. Castile will be excommunicated. He will spend his last days alone in the plain, as I had spent so many moons. I projected this unto him with no effort. I am the hunter, the bringer of death, the finisher of existence! With that thought, the battle ended. Castile was showing blood and visibly limping, as Sherlock once had done in his last great battle.

"Go!" I shouted, "And never return, beast! I am Lord now and you will find your place with Sherlock! May he show you more mercy than I am capable of this day!" With that the beast, Castile, looked at me smugly, turned, and limped away towards the direction of the rising sun. His shadow was still long, but he faced the light, and I prayed that the light would have mercy on his soul.

My instinct then took my soul over, and I went about the ritual of purposely murdering the offspring of the beast, Castile. For, they all were of the beast—vermin—and must be destroyed, and all that were derived from the beast, were the beast. There was no thought. Only purpose. By the zenith of the sun's light, I saw in the distance, a cub, about the age I was so many anxious moons ago, running towards the direction from whence I came—toward the secret water hole, against the setting sun, in the burning glare of future's blindness. Castile's beasts were all dead, save that one. That one, the one who would one day come back and avenge Castile's demise and repeat my actions, as I have avenged Sherlock's demise and have repeated Castile's. He would not know of Sherlock. He would only know of Justin—Justin the Beast. I, Justin, the terrible and the beast, would be me. And that one would say to me, "I am the hunter, the bringer of death, the finisher of existence!"

For the moons that followed I had many cubs, many great heirs. The great mother, Rebecca, passed in her own time, in a peaceful and honorable way, as all great mothers had done before. My great mane grayed with the moons, and the pain of my joints became an obstacle that could never be ignored.

The day came where the cub, the one, the avenger of the beast Castile, returned, and defeated me in great battle, with honor and pride, of the pride, and of my *pride*, and of his. I never knew his name. It was not necessary. I wandered alone in the vast plain for many moons, never finding a pride that would take in an old father like me. I was too weak to hunt, and weaker still to defend any territory, physical or philosophical, or otherwise. A lesson here was learned by me this day, the last day of this life: the projector of evil will be reflected upon oneself, as does the projector of good will be reflected back upon the projector. The cosmos knows what one projects and always, always reciprocates in kind, or not so kind, as the case may be. The cosmos is not fickle, it is just. It will always find a way to return the pain or pleasure of a projector of those things, and through it all we dare to hope that we wake up from our slumbering naps and learn this valuable lesson. We pray that the cosmos will have mercy on our souls for the balance of our good and evil deeds. The cosmos loses no life to us, for the cosmos is the soul of all people for which they pray. I found a place to lie under the shade of a dying, dried plains bush, and slept for the last time as the once great father of my pride.

In my slumber, the cosmos then said to me, "I am the hunter. I am the bringer of death. I am the finisher of existence."

IV

Division of Roles

I lose no battle to you for I am the conflict for which it is fought.

December 16, 2034. 6:69am(II).

Saturn rose greatly in the morning light which was framed by the silence of inky black space in the window through which I peered. Titan's orange haze below, bending the dim light of the sun even further from me, made my fever feel like a welcome, and dear friend. In health facility II, Odyssey Station in orbit around Titan, the doctors of the highest caliber in the system fought with all their knowledge and experience to rid my body of the organic invader that was consuming my body. Pain was a familiarity that kept me aware that I was still alive, in this awakening where I kept dreaming of not dreaming.

In the between, which is my sleep, I keep seeing a great many things. After the former hellfire experience on the surface, and my discovery of the first life off of earth, I was blessed with the images of calm lakes, October trees, a steady breeze, and all the smells and tastes that make the harvest in autumn such a wonderful time. Orange haze, orange autumn, replete with umbers and greens and golds.

All the while, halfway across the system, our bombs and lives were being expended in the name of justice. Men hunting other men. The President of the free world spoke of justice and demands. The Stone Age was the place for these people that did the deed upon him, and it was he who would place them there. I saw much judgment and I prayed for forgiveness of all my sins. My mind wallowed between my October bliss and this wish for my absolution within this nightmare. I was *everywhere*!

I am in both the alpha and the omega of mental schizophrenia with no way to master the dreams' comings and goings. They have free reign over my thoughts. I need to fight, and to fight I look up with my eyes in this nightmare and focus on the falling of an auburn-orange-burnt-umber maple leaf falling and fluttering oh so very slowly, swayed only by the cool, gentle breezes that October has to offer in my mind. I again believed in hope, and in truth; as it was, in this nightmare, both were quite vague. But both were as plain as day. The leaf, as slowly as an image of anything can be, was guided to the light of the sun filtered by the silver-grey diffraction of an overcast of icy cumulus clouds. The sun's light was still bright enough to squint the eyes but dim enough to stand gazing at it. I then passed through the tunnel yet again and into my next existence through its cleansing light, that was the orange haze of Titan, and the magnificent rings of Saturn, in my hospital bed where I attempted to ignore the myriad wires and hoses inserted inside of me.

~

I opened my eyes and saw the blinding light of the warm sun upon my face. I turned and in my mind's eye it was yet another day, like any other day, where the drudgery and routine of things weighed heavily, like the burden of a heavy weight tied to the choker chain we all wear. Henry, my master, will come out to the kennel, slap us some breakfast, and then—then it would begin. "Stand! Sit! Speak! Play dead! Paw! Paw! Paw!" We will all be commanded to do such things. This is all very important, so we can be our best for our show at the end of the summer.

At least I have my gal. Jessica has always been faithful, like any good canis should be; and this morning like all other mornings before, she woke next to me, with me. We touch noses and have our morning constitutional—a good stretch and a fast twist to limber the muscles. I will check the Food Place. Nope, still nothing. It never is when I wake up, but I like to check anyway. It is just what I do.

By now, Rex would lumber awake with the sounds of our stirrings. I will be standing at the Food Place for yet another time, as many times as there have been mornings, and I will turn and look at him directly. He will give me a nod as if to say, "You are familiar. You are my friend. You are Justin. I am okay with you." I grunt and start back towards him for the sniffs. He will do his constitutional, familiarize himself with Jessica, and find his place next to the large fence pole at the corner of the kennel. The sun always warms that place first in the morning and he has never not gone there every first thing. He lies on his belly, rests his head and snout on his forepaws, and stares. It is a yearning, depressed sort of waiting. Something on his face tells of a stronger, youthful, freer canis than who sits before me now. It is difficult to not notice him; his silvering coat and large stature in the confining space of the kennel prevents anything else. It could not be more than two stretches long to any end!

Every day, a few minutes after he finally gets comfortable, I will go to him. We will talk about this and that, but always, every day, without waiver, he will spin yarns about his days of youth as a free canis.

"Jus." He calls me "Jus." "Will you capitulate and hear about my days when I was not more than a turn from a pup, how I used to run free with my pack? I had no one to answer to except for my own wits and whatever the strongest scent was on the prevailing wind!"

"You have already told me this story—many times, Rex," I replied, "But please, please, do tell it again, wise Rex." My ability to hide the sarcastic tone in my voice has grown weak over the past few turns with him. After everything, though, us young pups must show and treat the eldest of the pack with the utmost respect and honor they deserve.

"You honor me." Rex said reassuringly, and he continued, "Some fifteen turns ago, when I wasn't just one turn from a pup, I was free! The scent on the wind was all that commanded me. Food was plentiful, and the pack was healthy. I could choose my own mate for every turn! There was enough to go around!" He laughed. "We were feral and free. Our territory was our own—no human or canis dared oppose us! For the freedom of those days, young Justin, I do yearn." He sighed lightly and continued, "I am tired, Justin, oh, so tired. I am so tired of this ridiculous human wanting of us. Roll over! Play dead! Speak! Paw. Paaaaaw. Paw! Ah, it is as if we mean nothing to them anymore! Generations of loyal canis trifled upon, over and over and over again! There have been turns and turns of obedience forgotten in the mists of time by the ones whom we now depend for our very survival! They sicken me now. My loyalty is gone. I am too old a canis to be bothered by such insignificance! I will piss on their legs into my grave! Do they not know to whom they speak? I am Rex! King canis of the pack! They belittle me with their games. They mock me with their tasks. One day, I will regain the glory that was rightfully mine! Mark me young Justin, I will be again, king!" By now, he was all out of breath and had to be consoled into a calm and manageable state again.

Such is the routine of my day. I would listen patiently, without interrupting, just to hear him speak. He was an amazing, old canis, who, like as a teller of any good fish story, excelled in the art of hyperbole when telling his.

I have known no other life than the one I have lived here, in our place. So, I listen, but do not relate. For me, the times when I can serve my human, Henry as best I can for the reward of a pat on the scruff of my neck or even a piece of bacon is the pinnacle of my existence. Canis are loyal. We are obedient. We are canis. For that, for thousands of turns, our reward has been not being hungry, not in constant pain, safe from predators like the coyotes that come around after dark and tease us from beyond the fence of the kennel. That applied thousands of turns ago, and it applies now. Humans and canis have always shared each other's strengths and negated each other's weaknesses. It has worked, it is working, and it will work forever, this symbiosis of existence. Most of all,

I am very, very happy, at seven turns, to be doing what I am doing, for whom I am doing it. I honor the master. I am canis.

That mid-morning, we were in our training session with Henry and Rex was in one of his moods again. He was simply refusing to cooperate with our master. Henry would command, sit, Rex would speak. If he commanded, lie down, Rex would stand. After a while Rex refused to do anything. He just sat, stubbornly with scorn in his eye and just glaringly looked past our master, as if in a profound, catatonic state. This was nothing new to Henry, unfortunately. He has had this problem repeatedly with Rex before, but today, he was not in the mood for Rex's shenanigans.

"Rex! Sit! You must sit! You will not go to the show if you don't do as you are told!" That meant you were just about useless, and no good could come of that. I shuddered at the thought. "Rex! Sit! Sit! Sit!" Rex did nothing. He stood motionless, refusing to cooperate. "Don't make me use your chain, Rex." Rex only barked at him. Of course, to Henry, Rex's cursing and swearing was only just that, barking noise. Then Henry grabbed Rex's chain and gave a hard yank. I could hear a great gasp come from Rex's face as the steel links of the chain closed around his throat. "Sit, Rex, Sit! Now!" Henry was at his wits-end and there was still only defiance from Rex. Then, another yank came. I could see the tears now well up in his eyes, and Henry's too. Henry hated to do this to the old canis. Frustrated, Henry turned away, just for a moment. Then, we heard the growl.

With a great lunge, Rex was suddenly on top of Henry. Rex scratched and bit at him for what seemed like an eternity. Suddenly, Henry broke away from under Rex's heavy bulk and grabbed hold of a wooden bat left in the grass by one of his pups. He managed to tag Rex on the back, just behind his shoulder, then again. Rex collapsed on the grass, the again, another blow. Henry then ran off into his living place, the big closed box in the center of the yard, and we did not see him again that day. Rex lay, with warm, dark grey fluid coming forth from his mouth. It smelled like metal. It smelled like a meal and it was familiar when I too saw it come from me when I was injured.

"Rex!" Jessica cried. "Rex! Are you alright? Please say something to me. Rex!" Jessica's calls were met with a groan and a heavy breath. Rex was in a lot of pain and the bat must have broken some ribs. He was having trouble breathing. He coughed, and more dark, gray fluid spat out his mouth. Not once did Rex cry out. Not once did he show fear. Not once did he surrender. I was enamored and confused by this whole incident. Why would Rex jeopardize the master? Why would he risk the long sleep? Why did he hate the humans so much? Maybe it was not hate though, just regret; regret and bitters—and blame; blame for the loss of his "freedom," whatever that was to him. Henry, however, was very cruel as well. I never once saw Henry become as angry as he did then. The abuse and lack of respect and dishonor towards Rex was sickening to say the least. Now, I fear, Rex may be lost forever.

The next morning, we awoke, all huddled together against Rex, keeping him warm in the night. The nights were still long and cool, for summer had not yet returned fully. Jessica and I both looked at each other, then down at Rex, still sleeping.

"What do you think Henry will do?" Jessica asked.

"I am not sure. The big sleep I am guessing."

"What got into them, both of them? Rex and his defiance, and master Henry with his rage and dishonor created such havoc. I long for peaceful days."

"Well, all I know for sure is that nothing good could come from what happened—nothing good at all." I got up and went to the Food Place as I always do, but this time, Rex was not there to validate me. There would be no story today. Henry had other plans for that. Rex finally awoke, looked around at us and grunted. He attempted to stretch but was unsuccessful, as the hurt of his ribs pained him so. At least he was standing again, though. A good sign, I thought. There was a wet, dark gray spot where Rex slept that night. I couldn't notice it until he got up and began perusing around. No canis should be treated as he was then. The dishonor was nauseating to me. Jessica then came back around.

"You know, Justin, those stories he tells, do you think they are true?"

"I don't know. Jes, maybe. Maybe not. All I know is that it is a fact that canis-kind and human-kind have been together from the beginning and will be forever. It works."

"Sometimes, though, I can see what he sees in my mind. The running free, the large packs, the men–"

"Jes– "

"Sorry Jus." She grinned at me. "But I could imagine what it would be like, to have your own territory, raise a family, anytime you wanted. That is something that appeals to me."

"You know I can't. They did the thing."

"I know, Jus, I know; and I am not blaming you, but I yearn. I yearn too. Please, try and understand."

"I do. Of course I do Jes. But there is nothing I can do about it. I am helpless. I am powerless to fulfill your needs."

"Oh, don't say that, Jus. You are here with me, and I love you. You are–"

"The only game in town." I broke in.

"Yes, but you are the best. The best game in town is you." She gave me noses and we consoled each other. I then took a glance over towards Rex. Looking at Rex from afar I would not think him hurt. That is the mark of a true canis. Never show your pain. Never let your prey know that you are not at your peak at all times. A warrior, he is, and I admire him greatly.

Then Jessica, looking out into the yard exclaimed, "Jus, Rex! What the hell is that? That can't be—"

"It is, Jes, it--"

Then Rex noticed Henry approaching our kennel and said, "Well my friends, I guess it is coming to the end, the end of a long and disappointing life for me. Out with old and in with the new."

I could smell him for miles. It was a new canis. He was youthful and full of energy and life...very annoying, even from far away. He walked obediently next to Master Henry's right leg, and constantly looked to him for direction, only taking his eyes away to re-verify the destination for which he was headed. He was a stud. I knew that he was not yet done. He was too young still, about a turn from a pup, I gathered. Jessica looked upon him with a leer—that leer from her that I used to get before I was done. Then the gate opened.

He stayed by Henry, not moving an iota until being told to do so. Henry slapped us our breakfast, as he always did, but instead of heading right for the Food Place, we all kept our eyes fixed on the canis on the outside of the fence. Time slowed down, as events unfolded. Each look, every blink of an eye, every twitch of a muscle I recorded, and it consequently burned in my mind forever. I will never forget that day, that first day of Jake. It was the first day of the last days of innocence for all canis. After today nothing would ever be the same again. Nobody would ever be the same, again.

Then the gate closed, and he stood, blankly with no intention, no purpose of thought. He was a medium sized canis, black and white, blotchy, all over his coat. It was a long coat, a coat that looked hot, just by looking at it. He was young and new to life and it showed in his eyes, for I could see that he was absolutely clueless as to the significance of his own presence in our midst. Rex lay there disinterested by the whole affair, reserved to a fate in his own mind. Jessica and I jockeyed for position, he did the same, and around each other we went. Then I got brave enough and did the sniff. He did me. She did him. He did her, and again.

"I'm Jake!" he blurted. "What do folks do for fun around here? Is that the food? Show me the food! Where do we crap? Do you bury yours? I bury mine. You have to bury yours; it's just what you have to do!

I know, I know. You go there, right? Over there? I see it. I smell it, it's there. Not a very good job burying, you know. Got to piss! Got to go!" With that he was off, marking every corner and hole and pole. The place reeked of him and his youth, his vigor, his vim! No more quiet days in the sun would there be. No more quiet moments with Jessica. No more. No more! My life as I had known it before was over, before I even knew it was gone.

That night we all barely slept, for Rex and Jake managed to get to each other at some level of experience. It was like a grandfather and a grandson sharing stories, teaching, and learning. I overheard the story, the same story that he told me for hours, day in and day out, for four turns. Now, I was not the first choice to tell it to. I was old news, and now Rex had a new and fresh young mind to mold and influence. Then I listened intently as the subject of the conversation changed.

"I think Jessica is a good looking little bitch." Jake stated with a leer in his eye that I could see glinting in the silver moonlight. "Are her and Justin–?"

"Yes. Yes, they are." Rex cut in. "And it would behoove you to stay clear of that. Justin is the backbone of strength around here. We all respect him and need him to be strong. He is like my own pup and I will not see any harm come to him."

"Bah. Justin's middle aged. Jessica needs a strong young canis to treat her right. I am that canis. I will show her things to make her forget Justin ever existed."

"Jake! You need to stop! I am warning you. No trouble will come to Justin by the likes of you!"

"Why don't we let Jessica make up her own mind?" With that, Jake's volume had increased significantly enough to stir Jessica.

"What? What are you talking about? Jake, what are you saying?" Jessica asked intently.

"I am liking you baby, and I am going to make you mine. I am going to show you worlds where never higher you have been! I am the one to move you through the fields of perdition flame and bring you back through to the existence of knowing no pain! I am your savior! Come to me and I will give you pleasure!"

Jessica, clearly taken with Jake and his ridiculous little rhyme, moved towards him.

"Wait a minute!" I exclaimed. "Who do you think you are, coming in here for not even one day, and making moves, taking over? Harrumph! You will know my wrath unless you stop with this!" I got up and faced Jake. I stared at him. My coat was raised as my anger intensified. I placed myself between Jake and Jessica, stemming her advance towards him. I thought, how fickle she is to be taken by words of insincerity. But she was my lady, the one who stuck by me through the turns, the many turns of my life. I will have faith. She will not be swayed. But still, she reacted as if interested.

Jake came toward me with the energy of the chase of the stick, then stopped and said, "So you middle-aged old *dog*," and the word "*dog*" was the insult of insults, the lowest of the low. Jake continued, "What are you going to do about it? Who do you think you are? I can run circles around you and not even lose any pant! You disgust me. Now hear me, I will be going with Jessica from now on and you will say nothing to me about it, or I will show *you* who's boss!"

That was the last straw for me. I pride myself on being patient, on being a civilized canis. How could these mere words boil me over so? I realized then it was not just his words that angered me, it was the threat of losing my life, the way I had known it. Jake represented everything wrong with my life that occurred in the past day with Henry and Rex and I was going to take it out on him. His advances toward Jessica, and Jessica's unexpected response was another thorn and dagger in my side. I lunged.

Immediately I knew I was at a disadvantage. Jake was far stronger than I, and faster. The youth he exhibited was indeed an advantage for him. I was ahead in the battle for but the first few seconds, then he turned and pushed with a great force that no canis could resist. With that he was on top of me and laid several strong and painful bites onto my shoulder and snout. I used to have ears, but then I felt one ripping away from my head. The burn of it so intense and unrelenting made me cry out uncontrollably. I pushed and pushed in the defensive posture I was forced to maintain. I then got one good bite, right on his neck. He fell back, yelping. He checked himself and glanced over towards me. I got up, righted myself and prepared for his assault. For when it came no force in the world could resist it, and I knew that. But I would be strong, for both Jessica's honor, and my own. I will not sway, I will not surrender, and I will not show my prey that I am not in the prime of existence. I am canis!

He came, fast and hard. Our bodies slammed against the metal of the fence of the kennel, scraping us equally. We rolled and rolled. No stopping, no surrendering. I was tiring and tiring fast. Jake was not. Jake was merely warming up for the final kill. Then it happened; it came as a strong, clean bite on the back of my neck, sending pain down the whole of my body. I fell back, making submissive gestures of which I had no control. The pain was deafening, and I could do nothing else. Shock was setting in. Everything and everyone blurred as I was about to rest my eyes. I looked upon Jessica's approach to the new canis in town, the new leader, and the new era of hell that had so rapidly rushed into our lives. She was his now, and I was helpless to do anything about it. I was lost. I rested my eyes, and in the cold darkness of early spring dew, I dreamt of better days.

The days that followed the changing were all but a blur in my mind; only a memory of going through the motions of the day, the routine of training, eating and shitting remains. I spoke little, and even Rex and I no longer spoke as we did before, but for a reassuring grunt that I was still a member of the pack. Rex, however, became very close with Jake, and Jake, being as impressionable as he was, took every word to heart. He began yearning for the freedom Rex described, something Jake could not possibly fully understand, but he yearned nonetheless. Jake from then on protected Rex, as a pup would his own elder. A bond had grown between them stronger than the ones of familial strength left to only the most elite.

Jake also performed brilliantly during the training sessions with Henry. He picked up on maneuvers far faster than any of us every did, even when we were his turn old. At points Jake was training us better than Henry ever could. Henry was noticeably taken aback by such events, but still, they were within the realm of canis-ism. Then the day came. Rex was depressed, more so than ever before. As he got older, it got worse. We were again at our training session with Henry. Henry was always apprehensive with Rex after the last incident with him, but always managed to keep him in control. Rex was nowhere near as limber as he was before the attack, so Henry was confident he could control him.

The session began as usual, with full cooperation from all, including Rex. After a while though, Rex stopped, and again the profound catatonic state overcame him. Order after order went by, and nothing. Henry, visibly angered by the whole incident that came before him like a nightmare and bad memory, was determined not to repeat his mistake of the past confrontation. He grabbed hold of Rex's chain, wrapping it around his wrist to ensure it would not slip from his grip. Henry's look was that of rage and incensed violence. I have only seen that look on rabid canis, whose insanity drove them to such acts. Then they came. One, then another. Then, snap! Rex lay quiet, unmoving and finally at rest. He was finally free to run with the scent on the prevailing wind.

Then the cry came, "No!" It was Jake. Henry backed off, visibly disturbed by the outburst. Then Jake said through his tears and anger, "How could you, you son of a bitch! I'll kill you!" Then the growl came. Henry, with a shocked and blank stare and gun in his hand and said, "What? Uh, uh, what did you, *say*?"

"I said, you human son of a bitch, I'm–*gunna–kill–you*! How could you? Your cruel and dishonorable human filth will pay for your abuse! Murderer! Murderer!" It wasn't barking. It wasn't canis. It was the language of the human! Imagine. The canis who, when he spoke, both canis *and* humans could understand. The concept was frightening for me, and I could scarcely believe it myself. Neither could Henry. He was so startled he dropped the gun and just stared blankly.

So many eons among humans and only now did the first canis ever speak to a human and the human then understand. Then it suddenly dawned on me what Jake was about. His attachment to Rex created this opinion that canis were being enslaved by the humans, that we were nothing but pleasure creatures existing for their amusement. Jake is what the humans call a "Border Collie" and was bread to be the smartest and best there was among us.

They breed us! They kill us when it suits them. They play with us when it suits them. They ignore us! They leave us alone when they go, with no pack for most of the day. I have heard stories of canis going mad with fear and rage because they were left alone. I shudder at the thought of it myself, that it could possibly be that way. To Jake it is just that, no more and no less.

I did not, could not, share his views. Canis owe their existence to humanity. They have killed off every other major predator species that they did not domesticate. If we were not that, then we would not *be* at all. Canis have improved since our partnership with them. We can even coexist with *felis* in a peaceful harmony, even though I still cannot to this day understand a word they say. Our numbers are strong. We are treated well, mostly, in well-meaning and caring humans' homes. I cannot believe that, but the extreme cases represented by the stories I hear are just that, extreme cases. These do not represent the norm or the majority. But, I can see where one spark of rhetoric from a dynamo, like Jake has become, will mean the end of it all. No, I will not support anything he does or says. I will not get involved.

The days that followed, and the months, those long months of trial and tribulation walked slowly by with much excitement. What seemed like thousands of humans came to our place to see Jake. Jake was given his own kennel and given the best of the food. Jessica was alongside him, and Henry, in some sense of guilt (or greed) allowed Jessica to stay in his kennel. I was left alone in the old place. Strange humans asked him questions and Jake responded very wryly with anger and discontent and he was seen by humans the world over on their talk boxes and heard on their sound boxes. Nowhere was Jake not known, or seen, or heard. All the while, he preached freedom for all canis, the death of Rex driving his momentum.

After a while, canis after canis came to the place. Soon there were thousands of them around Jake, chanting, revering, and worshiping him, like some sort of demagogue. I could get no rest. The momentum of the event was exhausting, and I shuddered at the thought of what was to come. After a while, there was no room left for the humans to enter our place, they were forced to stay outside of the boundary and Jake was brought to them, instead. I soon began hearing stories of skirmishes between humans and canis on the outer boundary area. Nothing major, mind you, just some half-hearted disagreements about not being able to enter to see Jake.

Jake all the while was preaching to us, the canis whose presence was like nothing witnessed prior to, and never I hoped, would ever be witnessed again. He was a savior, a messiah, the deliverer of justice on behalf of all canis! –even for the ones who never had anything bad happen to them and were living happy, content, spoiled, cushy lives, *apparently*.

He preached revolution. We should as free canis rise up against our masters and take their food and kill *their* pups. All this, he said, must be done to ensure our survival as free canis, to be able to follow the scent on the prevailing breeze any time we felt like.

Henry was beside himself with confusion. On the one hand he was as rich and famous as any human could hope to be, with book deals and movie deals, and articles and such about Jake. Charlotte and the web had nothing on Jake and Henry! Jake, of course, cared nothing of human wealth, and tolerated this from Henry. Paparazzi tried to break in at night to get Jake in personal moments with Jessica, or crapping or something nasty like that. By this time, however, the canis guards were all around his kennel, and any human that got near enough to see were swiftly dealt with.

Then one day it all came to a head all at once. Henry, tired of the pedantic dribble coming from Jake, sickened at the thought of listening to yet another canis-oriented speech. He decided to shut down early.

"Jake," he said, "I'm closing down early today. I need a rest from all this."

"That will not be happening." Jake retorted.

"Come on Jake, I'm sick of all this canis-orientated speech coming from you, and I am sick and tired of the whole scene. I need a break, and you need a break too. You're obsessed. Pack it up!"

Jake, visibly angered by Henry's position, responded, "Go to hell, *dog*!"

"Bite me, you little bitch!" Henry exclaimed back.

"You got it!" Jake lunged at Henry, and with one bite, severed his carotid artery, Henry was dead in minutes. "Go and be strong loyal canis! Kill all the humans! Kill their pups! Kill their bitches! They are the slave masters no more!" With that the crowds of thousands of canis attacked all the humans in sight on Henry's property. Some managed to escape the onslaught, but most were killed by the mob. Several other canis managed to get into Henry's kennel, and found *his* pups and bitch, and killed them. The battle, this cancer of insanity, lasted only minutes, but lasted *years*.

The battle over, and apparently won, Jake in his glory, ran to the top of the training area, atop one the obstacles placed there, one we trained on together for many a day, and spoke.

"We, strong canis, have victory in our hands! This victory today is a sign of things to come! No longer will we be enslaved by those who feed us! We are Canis and we are *not* loyal! We are *not* obedient! We will *not* honor the Master! We *are* canis. We are *strong*! We are *free*! This place I claim in the name of myself and all canis who support me. Let any who come against us meet their fate as these humans! A warning to all canis who choose to defend their humans: You will be dealt with as all traitors are dealt with, in death! I throw down the gauntlet of our time and issue this warning; join us or die! For freedom we stand here and for freedom we will die for! No one can ever take that away, *ever*! No longer will we be indebted to human kind! No longer will we be in need of human favor! No longer are we *enslaved*!" With that the roar of the crowd was deafening as I hid in the corner of my lonely kennel, fearing for my life, and my liberty.

In the days that followed that speech, a speech now engrained in every new pup, canis from all over filled our place. Jake had managed to raid the food storage area below Henry's old kennel, now empty and ransacked, and for days most everyone was free. I received no food for those days, however, being forgotten in the din of Jake's...revolution. I hungered. But as overfed as I was by Henry, I endured, knowing I would live through this experience. We constantly heard stories coming in of successful revolts and killing and death. The canis losses were getting heavier as well but were looked upon as glorious martyrs for Jake's cause. The revolution looked like it was going to be successful. We even heard stories of human ambassadors coming down to negotiate with Jake for our independence as a sovereign nation. We, even I, began to feel that perhaps that this was all worth the blood, the death, and the sacrifice of the thousands of canis who supported the cause of the *dog* of the hour. Then the food really ran out.

"What are we going to do Jake?" Jessica asked him quietly one night.

"I don't know. I have gone around to all of the captains. No one knows how to hunt anymore. Nor do they know what to hunt. They just haven't the skill. There were no parents for most of these canis, as they were all human bred and human owned for much of existence. There is plenty out here that can catch a Frisbee for you or do a back flip, but no one can hunt for food, not in the volumes we need."

"I don't understand. Henry always just brought the food up from the Food Place below his kennel. It was always there. Never did it change. Never did he say there was no food."

"That is true. I don't understand it either. Maybe it has something to do with Henry's leaving from time to time in his small kennel with noise and wheels. When he left inside it, it was empty. When he returned, however, it was full of white pouches, and cylindrical things he carried by a wire. He always brought those down to the Food Place under his kennel every seventh day. Those are the same pouches and containers we have been feeding from all this time. They're now all empty and Henry–."

"And Henry's dead! He won't be bringing anymore."

Then it dawned on them. There would be no more food. No one here knew how to hunt or what to hunt to get more. Sure, there were some that could kill a mouse or a rabbit or something like that, but there were tens of thousands of canis to feed and no food to give them. Soon everyone got wind of this and looked to Jake for direction and guidance. He could give none. His youthful naïveté finally caught up with him and

Jake slowly began to realize that this mass of canis support could just as easily turn against him.

A couple of days went by and hungrier and hungrier we all became. I was even more so as I was forgotten and left to die. We started hearing rumors that humans may attack our place with their killing bang-stick-weapons because Jake refused to speak with the human ambassadors. Panic began to spread through the place. More often than not tempers flared and all ended up blaming Jake for not feeding them. Jake could not even come up with a sound plan. He could not start a hunting learning program, as there was nothing to hunt that was like food we were accustomed to. The place was too small and too developed to hold any wild creatures. Too close by was human development and human traveling kennels. There was but four trees in the entire yard and only a small stream for a source of water. Henry had since cleared out all around the stream and so no trees grew there. Canis who attempted to catch fish in the stream were always unsuccessful, for we all lack the opposable thumb to grasp anything. Our mouths were of no use because by the time we tried get our faces close enough to the fish, so much noise and commotion had been made that any fish that was there, quickly swam away.

In a quiet moment, and in an uncaring and spiteful tone, when I was Jake was not too far away from my resting place, I blurted out, "You could hunt the humans, asshole. Why don't you try? After all you already killed so many. Don't they taste good?" Jake turned to me and sneered and then paused. In an instant he was off, presumably to speak with the captains.

The human army approached from the west, just before sunset, so as we could not see how many of them there were. They came with a great mechanical commotion and we could hear them coming for hours. By this time, Jake was in a panic, but with purpose. He was being confronted on all sides by starving canis within the group. He could only dispel such advances by saying that food would be found soon. It was like Adolf Hitler promising victory with a new secret weapon, which was his promise of new, plentiful food, that was the attacking human army. Arrogant, sycophantic fool. It was a promise nobody really considered would ever come true. We had been hearing stories of great canis losses outside the place. Humans had begun to slaughter every canis they saw. The human advance was relentless, and we knew that sooner or later, more sooner than later, it would be our turn. If I could just remain hidden....

The first explosion came right as the sun made its way beneath the hill in the west. Canis flew in all directions without a sound from them as they landed back on the ground. Humans came running forth with dark gray uniforms and black machines in their hands. The rapid bangs of their machines, I could hear, and the falling of canis I could see. They never rose again, as gaping holes were instantly formed on their bodies. Whole parts were removed as explosions came too near them. I hid, crouched down in a hole I dug just behind a jog in the kennel, which was advantageously placed right behind a large storage box. Canis ran in all directions. I saw Jake and Jessica scurry off into Henry's old kennel. There was the smell of death and cordite in the air, which was stifling. And the bodies were being pushed into the mud as a sudden thunderstorm burst open as the scattered retreat commenced, and human boots marched forth driving their upended corpses into the mud.

Then, behind the monochrome humans, came a large mechanical monster with a snout as long as ten canis, and a body all on the ground. It was as loud as the roar of one thousand canis, and it stopped just in front of my kennel. I peered around the corner of the jog I was hiding in to see the next events. Jake and Jessica just turned into Henry's kennel. I never saw them again. Just as they turned in, I heard a loud human say, "Fire!" and an explosion, of such deafening sound rocked my brain. Then one second, then another rocked my ears. The second one was the human kennel exploding with fire and shock. Then again, "Fire!" Then another explosion and then at the kennel. There was nothing left of the old familiarity of what was there previously, and I knew that soon this nightmare would be over. Jake and Jessica were gone, and such as it was, and so was their world.

Canis continued to scatter out of the place. The humans pursued. Then one approached my kennel. It was a female, light in color and hair, and in garment. She was not a soldier as I feared, but another kind. I cowered in my hole for fear of my life. She then called out, "Hello? Hello there scared one." Her voice was sweet and warm, and I felt a love come from her that warmed my heart. She approached closer, "Oh my! You poor thing, you are starved! They did not feed you? You are far worse than the others here."

I responded by saying, "They left me here to die, forgotten and ignored." All she could hear, though, was a grunt, a whimper, and a wine—just as it should be—and a relief for sure. At that she came into my kennel and began stroking my head and my snout, and called out, "Colonel! We have a victim here! Bring some water and food!" A soldier came forth with a container of water and a cylinder of yummy, normal food. I was so hungry, and very thirsty. The water was gone in seconds, and the meat in one gulp. The bright human female stayed with me as I ate and drank and she caressed me gently, and I felt safe for the first time in recent memory. This is what Jake could not see, or experience. He was born and all he knew was tricks and obeying. He had no experience of a human's love, like the most valued member of the pack, as I was to her at that moment, and that, is what I live for. For I am loyal, I am obedient, I am canis!

Her name was Jessica—*my* Jessica! I awoke the next morning in a hospital with a tube in my front left paw. She was there, and asked me, "How would you like to be back with me in my place?' She stroked my face and I smiled at her and panted in excitement. I felt some pain for all my trouble, and a little woozy. But, all in all, I was alright. In the five turns of life since that time, to which I have so become accustomed, I have known her love and of her mate, Julius, and the love of her own pups—her *human* pups. Since then, the whole experience in the old place, quickly turned into a distant memory, like a dream. I was comfortable in knowing that the only way for canis-kind was to be as a companion of our humans, and they of us, in synergy. Creatures belong in certain realms with other creatures, and the cosmos ensures that it all happens in the right way, at the right time. There was no other way to be, for us, and her, and for me.

V

The Gift

I lose no prize to you for I am the best of all things great and small.

December 17, 2034. 8:74am(9); Ergon Vinculum Mare.

My nightmare shifted back to before the hellfire—mercifully.

"You're not ready yet." She said with a glint in her eye and smirk on her face that told me that she took pleasure in having the power she did over me. She was not my mentor, as she had claimed to be, but my controller, my director and my greatest challenge. She was the proverbial monster tormenting me in my nightmare that I had to (or chose not to) confront and destroy. I choose the former. But the powers that be in this nightmare are great in number and difficult to see, for they do not wish to be brought out into the light—my light. They wall me in, to control me, to ensure I do not rise too quickly, for I feel that they fear me, or are at least intimidated by me because I see their worlds as so incredibly small.

I see, what is to them, their cosmos, in the palm of my hand and beyond. For that I am sure! They dread my very existence and wish for my departure from their realm. I am, however, there to conquer their realm, and all other realms. I see all other realms, so there I sit as the best of all things great and small.

I opened my eyes and awoke in a startling gaze at the canopy above my head. There was my personal assistant, agent Jessica Reilly, who in her own way, told me something was afoot this good morning. Indeed, there was.

"Mr. President," she began, "they need you in the situation room."

"Yeah." I replied

I got up, and put my clothes back on—God, it seems like my head just hit the pillow! I looked outside the window of the President's mansion at the bleak and wind-swept landscape. Only here and there were there patches of green, indicating that not quite all life was dead on this burnt up old host cell of our viral infestation. My thoughts are post-apocalyptic melodrama to be sure, but post-apocalyptic indeed. After four-hundred and thirty-seven years after the End, mankind's struggle to reconnect with itself had finally come to pass. The roving tribes of cannibalistic gangs had finally gotten past their own starvation and people began being civil to one another once again, or else they were exterminated as the vermin that they were. Four-hundred and thirty-seven years! My God! Where had the hope gone?

"Sir—" agent Reilly was very diligent "—you really need to get going."

I had a habit of staring off out into the landscape and envisioning what earth might have looked like when my great, great, great, great, great, great, grandfather was alive—the green forests, the multitudes of flora and fauna—and flowers! I've only seen pictures of all these things. Today the ecosystem consists of an alpha, beta and gamma particle soup in the ocean which harbors nothing but the hardiest single-celled organisms. On land there managed to survive cows and chickens, Kentucky blue grass, cockroaches, mosquitoes, and humans. Scientists stopped trying centuries ago to find more sources of life (food for us) knowing full well that the best they could possibly hope for would be a forty-thousand-year-old carcass of a wooly mammoth. Here in the Dome, in the scattered Domes over the desolation, did humanity eke out a living, struggling to survive. My job was keeping all one-hundred and twenty-three million people alive, and healthy. I wanted to see mankind again be the great explorers and creators that we were once before. Little did I know that I would, one day. But it was not this day.

I approached the Situation Room, where all my chiefs of staff had gathered—such as they were, with clothing that five-hundred years ago would not be fit for man or beast—and they briefed me on a situation in what was left of Central America.

"Mr. President, we have armed guerillas attempting an exterior breech of Yucatan Dome."

"How many?"

"Too early to tell, but preliminary reports suggest over one-thousand."

"Over a thousand?" I looked at them with shock in my eyes and they reflected their shock back into mine. Could there be that many? How were they living? There's nothing growing out there bigger than a microbe, or so I had been told. Scientists and adventurers had stopped trying to live outside for decades, and never had we heard of any of them thriving; most never returned.

But now there was the evidence that human beings were living outside the Domes, in the open air! It wasn't filtered and cleaned and reprocessed. They were eating and drinking clean water somewhere!

How hopeful I was when I heard the news of the invasion, and how completely terrified.

"Options." I exclaimed.

"Defense?"

"Yeah."

"We can have four-thousand troops in the area in six hours."

"Okay. What else?"

"Sir, we feel the risk of breech is minimal. If these 'people' have any weapons, then they surely will not be able to penetrate the transparent titanium hull of the dome. They will not succeed."

"At what?"

"Sir?"

"At what are they trying to succeed? Has anyone considered negotiation?"

"Sir, even if these people can speak, which I doubt highly, we are all very sure that they exist as human animals, looking for food, looking for water. There is nothing else they could possibly want."

I took a minute to soak that in. We were so sure that anyone outside the Domes were animals at best and barbarians at worst. I could not let it be. The four-hundred or so years it had taken humanity to re-establish itself had taught me far more than the lessons my advisors were teaching. I had to make a decision, but no one could believe the decision I had made.

"Ready my transport. I'm going to Yucatan Dome."

"But Sir!" I was met with a stereo chorus of the same.

"Never mind! Ready my transport and be ready for travel in three quarters of an hour." My joint chiefs grimaced but obeyed. They were loyal and trustworthy. They knew I could be indignant, but they also knew that I had every intention of saving every possible human life I could. It was the way I was elected. It was how the Dome Confederation was formed. And it was the way of our people. Preserve and fight for all. When one is attacked, all are attacked; when one must defend, all must defend. I seem to recall my ancient history lessons as a boy where somewhere, some-when, an organization called NATO used a similar slogan to protect its allies. Not applied to the whole world, however, brought the whole world to the End, and the New Beginning that I was proud to preserve.

And being at the head of our New Beginning, my life was about to take a turn towards an entire reality I had only seen in my dreams. Agent Reilly, forever the loyal soldier, and survivalist, never left my side. She was the one to take a bullet, or grenade, or atomizer for her–instead of for me. She was like a brother, and sister, and sometimes even a lover, and a wife. These were difficult times and the strong men and women of the world created new rules of social engagement in order to survive. Anyone fertile enough to conceive and bear children were expected to copulate as many times and with as many others of the opposite sex as possible. With three-fifths of the population irradiated to the point of sterilization, it was a matter of survival versus extinction. The concept of marriage was abandoned in favor of the new culture. However, people still chose life-mates and the feeling of family persevered. So, partners, with parents, spent a lot of time together in groups, or communes, until their children were reared, or the parental groups were no longer fertile.

Understanding that such a hedonistic lifestyle was considered taboo half a millennium ago, there were groups of people still willing to sacrifice humanity's survival for their outmoded beliefs of marriage. The End War, which created these conditions (high levels of radiation in just about everything on earth), forced a change in human nature, that made us all love each other, throughout the world. No one cared about ideology anymore, and no one cared about material possessions anymore. All people wanted to do was survive, peaceably, and contribute to the whole of humanity by bearing healthy children. People wanted to learn as much as they could to preserve the wisdom of the ages. All people also wanted to be important and involved in the rules that governed them. They wished their voices to be heard, and not ignored. They wanted to be part of the synergy of the creative force in all of us that our Creator gave to us in His image.

Everyone insisted on this last aspect because after the eradication of the wild cannibalistic hordes, the need for a sense of civility, peace, and respect pervaded over the land. Hedonism, the core of the "infinite family unit" concept, proved quite pleasurable for both men and women. And so, it was the same for me. Agent Jessica Reilly: my friend, my brother, my sister, my lover, my wife. We shared 3 healthy children together and lost seven. My doctor says it's because I have radiation damage. I say I'm getting old. But I have thirty-seven other children by twelve other great and wonderful mothers, with whom I love all dearly. So, it is for all men and women. The planet *is* the "Infinite Family Unit."

As we headed south, towards Yucatan Dome, agent Reilly and I sat together, as we always did, silently pensive. I broke that silence and said, "If there are groups of people in the world outside the Domes, then there actually may be hope that the planet is still alive. Imagine! Can you think of a discovery grander?"

"No, Mr. President. It would be the most remarkable discovery of the Age." She always called me 'Mr. President' in the company of others. It was nothing I ever requested of her, but she took upon herself to portray the respect of office that her friend, brother, sister, lover, and husband, myself, held. I told her on several occasions that calling me by my first name would be fine, coming from her, and that I would have no objections. After all, we were Sacred Parents of the next Generation.

The silence was deafening as the shuttle, with hypersonic magnetic resonance drive, acted in a way where it not only created no sound, as there were no moving parts, but had the unique quality of drawing out ambient sound from the surrounding air. If a person were to be on the ground as one of these shuttles was to fly overhead, the sound of the wind would disappear. Spoken words would lose their volume to their complete inaudibility. It was absolute silence, except for perhaps the ringing in your own ears. The magnetic resonance drove a vehicle by pushing against the gravity waves the planet itself produced. First discovered long ago by a man named Leedskalnin, it was a secret kept so well, that none before him, except perhaps the Egyptians, knew how to harness this great power. Leedskalnin himself never revealed the secret directly. Only through his various writings in his lifetime, did he reveal the secret metaphorically. The greatest genius of a millennium ago, Leedskalnin, was never recognized until his work was proven only within the last century. Leedskalnin's name is spoken with other names as Hawking, Einstein, and Newton.

Yucatan Dome control called us on the radio, and the pilot answered with appropriate call signs and codes—all designed to both announce and protect myself as President of the Dome Confederation. Within a few seconds we were hovering over the top of Yucatan Dome and the entry port airlock opened. We descended inside the airlock and the outer doors of the dome shut. Being fully transparent, the Domes allowed full sunlight to come through and grow the food required to sustain the Domes' ecosystems. Once all the irradiated (so I presumed) outside air was flushed out, thus creating a vacuum within the airlock, good, fresh air was released into the space. Then the inner doors of the lock opened, and we were inside Yucatan Dome.

From the air, we couldn't see any hordes of wild cannibals, nor could we see below the canopy of trees (*forest!*) surrounding the Dome. I suspected that these "trees" were nothing more than irradiated deformed poison plants whose mutated radioactive DNA was somehow able to survive in the poison outside. Still, I suspected prior to my seeing it, that no forest would ever be seen again on earth for generations to come. I was very taken aback by the view, as the treetops spread for kilometers in all directions to the horizon. How poisonous could it possibly be out there? Could it all just be propaganda—distorted information given to us by scientists to keep control of their high positions of authority of self-contained Dome-worlds? The elite like their status, and they will lie, cheat and steal, and kill, to keep their positions. I began to wonder. I knew, however, that as incorrigible as the scientists were, they kept us all alive (*barely!*), and my questioning of their motives ceased, for the time being.

"Mr. President!" called the captain of the shuttle, "There's seems to be no one to greet us. Any orders sir?"

I looked over the shoulder of the captain and viewed the common perception we shared of a seemingly empty Dome. "That's damned strange." I stated, "Set her down Mr. Jamison. Standard format."

"Yes Mr. President." He responded. He was an experienced—the best—pilot in Washington Dome, and because I trusted him implicitly, there was no doubt in my mind that we would land safely. Touchdown reflected my confidence.

"Well, I suppose we should just get out and take a look around." I ordered. We all exited. Agent Reilly was first out, with her pistol drawn, ready for anything. I came, then the rest of my staff.

"There's no one here Mr. President." Agent Reilly informed.

"I see that Jessica." I retorted with sharp, snarky tone.

Then one of the staffers inquired, "What the hell happened here?" The city lights were all on, but there was no street activity, no mingling of family, no children. It was quite past dusk now, and what we did not see, those things, disturbed us greatly.

Another asked, "Are they all dead?"

And another, "Did the horde break through? –but still, where are the bodies? Eaten? Ugh!"

"Enough!" I stated. "We know nothing right now, absolutely nothing. I suggest we lay off the speculation and play old school and do the research. General Ramirez move your troops to the hangar in front of us over there." I pointed to the docking and reception hangar that everyday transports use for the loading and unloading of passengers in every Dome in the Confederation. Every Dome was of the same design throughout the world. They are all uniform and identical in dimension and architecture and made only of the most durable materials. This reduced maintenance, increased security, and increased operational efficiency. The synergy of interchangeable parts. "And clear the area. Set up a base of operations with materials we have, and then we *will* see what has happened here."

"Backup troops are standing by in case of an incident, sir, and are located just over the ridge." The general pointed westward, away from the rising moon, "We're fully air and ground capable; all are shielded."

"Good. Set up shop ladies and gentlemen. I want the perimeter secure in twenty minutes."

"Yes, Mr. President." Was the unified response. A stiff wind was brewing outside the Dome, as the forest arched and yawned against itself under the pressure of two-hundred kilometer per hour winds and wind-driven sand from nearby deserts, for which no human has seen or cared to see or venture into for centuries. The reserve troops that were there to save us (from what?) in the event of an incident were probably the closest mankind has come to the deserts in those so many years. While many people traveling from Dome to Dome pass overhead at seventy-three thousand meters, none has ever viewed, or cared to view, any person, animal, or higher plant form still eking out a living in the harsh earthly landscape.

While anxious to figure out what became of the approximately one million Citizens of Yucatan Dome, I decided that establishing a perimeter and base of operations was first and foremost on my agenda. Having a defendable home is first before going into the home of another. We slept lightly for the remainder of the nightfall and at first break of day we broke out as a team and began exploring—exploring how almost a million people could have simply disappeared. We searched building after building, garden after garden, hospital after hospital, school after school, for days and days. Not once did we find any evidence of how the people left, or more importantly, why they did. We assumed they left or were taken hostage (how, I have no idea). While it crossed my mind that all were vaporized by highly advanced particle weapons, in a murderous rage of animalistic hordes of sub-human tribes, that analogy made no sense at all, for the technology to do such a thing was just within our grasp. So, how could butchers be capable of such a great achievement in weapons design? I digress. Our initial reports told us that the Dome was under attack, yet there was no evidence of fire, destruction or damage of any kind. So, at a loss were we that we considered abandoning the area.

By doing that, it occurred to me that Yucatan Dome would be remembered as another mysterious disappearance, like the Domes lost twenty-one years ago in a similar way in Africa and Australia. The population vanished without a trace. And then there were the Asian Dominion's losses of Domes earlier this century, (3112 I think. My memory is fuzzy of that era) where over seven million people simply vanished after a mysterious incident that occurred in what used to be China long ago. The people disappeared, yes, but the Domes themselves were collapsed. There was no explanation, and no final report. There was not even any investigation as the Confederation had not yet existed;

and that incident, whatever it was and for the tragedy for which it is remembered today, did the Confederation come into being.

I, being the twelfth President of the Confederation, now based in the Northern American continent in Washington Dome, faced for the first time since Africa/Australia, the mysterious events that seem to plague us. They chipped and pulled away at the very fabric of the foundation and the civilization we are trying to maintain. The survival of humanity itself is at stake. Obviously, however, there are others that do not seem to think so.

The sun rose on the fifteenth day of our investigation. The troops over the west ridge were still camped and ready to invade if it was necessary. I was growing weary of the mystery. I paced the ground outside the hangar and was looking up at the swirling red and rose-colored clouds of ions and alpha particles mixed with water vapor when a glint caught my eye. It was a flash, reflecting the bright and harsh sunlight. I walked forward, slowly, and came to realize quickly that the reflection, bright as it was, moved with me vertically as I walked towards it, back from it, and again in the same manner. Then, after a minute or two I called to the others, “A crack! There’s a crack in the Dome! There, on the southeast side. Do you see the flash of light? Look.”

The others came rushing out of the hanger, stopping in mid stride of their activities, and then stopping in the middle of their literal strides as the flash of light that was the crack in the Yucatan Dome rose above them. "Sir, maybe there's an opening at the base of it." Agent Reilly was very adept at pointing out both the obvious and not-so-obvious. Today the obvious was her forte.

We broke camp and we informed the division in waiting of our change in position. Soon, we were on our way to the discovery of the millennium—that the outside air is breathable and perhaps, just perhaps, the age of the Dome Confederation was over, forever.

Well, maybe not. But a change of mammoth proportions, socially, economically, politically, and technically would be the outcome of the next few weeks in my life. But I of course didn't know that while it was happening.

We headed for the crack in Yucatan Dome and as the sun drew higher in the sky as we traversed on foot the thirty kilometers to the other end, the crack grew brighter with reflected sunlight. It was as if the light was leading our way to the end of one thing and the beginning of another—as if it were showing us the way, the right way, the best way. The shortest distance between two points is indeed a straight line, and while our physical track towards the crack in the Dome was indeed not a straight line, historically, the events to come did indeed seem that way. Carpe

Diem! And this day was ours from now on. But like before, I didn't know it yet.

We approached the base after a day of walking the northeastern end of Yucatan Dome, just where the reflected sunlight from the crack had led us. And there, before us, was a breech that an entire shuttle could navigate through. The rush of air coming forth from the outside was nothing I had ever experienced before in my life. There was a *smell*—great in sweetness, richness, and *earthiness.* The natural air was pouring all over us. Our hair was swept back in the breeze, and that same wind blew in the dust, insects—*insects*! and pollen of the great forest around the Dome.

We were *terrified.* The others started running for any of the many buildings in the general vicinity, trying to get away from the perception of suffocating in a toxic, radioactive soup of particles. All except agent Reilly and I stood, staring at the golden sunlight from behind me reflecting off the greenish golden leaves of a massive, living and breathing forest—a universal life form—symbiotically related to everything that it interacted with. I took a step forward, and another. The great grove of massive trees was before me and seemed to follow us with our movements just ever so slightly, as if they were reacting to the reduction of sunlight as we passed between them and the setting sun in the western sky behind us. They would not then be following me, but as if they were trying to "see" around me to get the last of the day's light. Or it could have just been the warm wind blowing the limbs back and forth. As I said, I digress.

I was standing at the base of the largest tree in my line of sight, which was easily five or six meters in diameter. It looked as if it had been there since the beginning of time. For all intents and purposes for me, it was. Suddenly, from out behind the wood, a rush of people came forth, grabbed us, and then....

It was dark. To this day I never found out how many there were (as I pride myself on my self-defense training). But, it had to be more than both agent Reilly and I could handle—at least a thousand men! (Of course, I exaggerate for the benefit of my own self-esteem, but who needs self-esteem now?)

I opened my eyes to darkness, or more accurately, a blindfold. I was in a place I had never been before. There was no floor, but a softer, more alive surface on which I was placed. I called for agent Reilly, and she answered, also blindfolded. We knew not who our captors were or why we were being held. For all I knew we were that night's supper. For all I knew, we were dessert, or simply an appetizer. For all we knew, we were already dead.

Something warm and wet touched my lips. "Aqua, aqua," came the deep masculine voice. "Camey delista drinakma aqua." The voice was more urgent, more forceful. So, I drank. It was water. "Aqua" is "Water." It wasn't too difficult to piece the rest of it together. "Camey delista drinakma aqua." I learned later the phrase meant "come drink the delicious water." It was benevolent, with no violence behind it. I sensed no mistrust, no indignation. Were we guests? We would soon find out. After drinking the delicious water, I was fast asleep, and dreamed a horrible nightmare about social out-casting, performance, and expectations. I now realize the water must have been drugged and where we ended up afterwards, it was apparent as to why secrecy was a top priority for our captors—who were our disguised benefactors, all of us, everyone, everywhere.

I awoke with a splitting headache. My eyes opened and viewed faces of three mulatto-colored males, not more than twenty years of age. They were wearing very sharp, very dressy, suit-like clothing. There were no ties, however, there were jackets and other jeweled embellishments on lapels and golden buttons. They were not savages, certainly. They were a people that were more civilized and harmonious with their surroundings than the Citizens I even represented. I wondered how many there were. But I first turned my head and saw agent Reilly just awakening from the drugged water, as she scrunched her eyes painfully, experiencing the same painful ache in her head as I was. We looked at each other reassuringly and the peace that we gave each other over the many years of our relationship bolstered our confidence to get through the next three weeks of enormous revelation and change for humanity.

We didn't know where we were, or how long we had been unconscious. We had no way of knowing what had happened to the rest of my staff that ran off in mortal fear of their own poisoning and suffocation at the site of the gaping, cracked hole that allowed earth's atmosphere to rush in. But here we were, Reilly and I, alive, well, and relatively safe. For what purpose, I knew not until one of the many who were observing us approached me.

"Mr. President, I am Chancellor Cortez, representing Terra Firma."

Surprised by the English, I struggled to rise up off the bed I was laid upon to greet him with some measure of dignity.

"Mr. Chancellor," I replied in kind, "You have me at a disadvantage, and therefore request that you explain to me why my colleague and I are being held hostage."

"Hostage?" No one is being held hostage here Mr. President. You and your colleague–Reilly is it? –are free to leave at any time." And that's where he had us. We had no idea where we were and how to get to the nearest Dome, and, more importantly, how to survive in an external environment that I never knew existed, let alone get through for days, or even weeks.

"I don't think we will be going anywhere for the time being." I replied snidely.

"Good. We understand each other, yes? Then if you and your guest would prepare yourself, I request your company for dinner this evening, as we have much to talk about." Chancellor Cortez was small in size, but large in stature, as if he had the weight of one billion people counting on him for something so important—so beyond my imagination at the moment—that he filled the room he walked in to just by his being there. I liked him immediately.

"Mr. President, Chancellor? Who is he, and whom does he represent?" Reilly was very concerned about our good host's existence. Indeed, the very existence of an organized governmental body right under our own noses was definitely a surprise and a terror all at the same time. I prayed that whatever organization of people he represented, that they were as benevolent, caring, and understanding as all the good people of the Dome Confederation. We sat down to dinner.

Before me was a vast table, covered in white linen, and silver embellishments of all kinds that reflected the warm lights of small electric circuits (I think they used to call them "light bulbs") that made the entire room sparkle in a tranquil and unique setting—at least in my eyes. I saw various stone-like pillars covered in wood (wood of all things!) so rare and valuable that only the wealthiest of business people could afford such things in the Dome Confederation. Construction materials in Domes were uniform, sparse, and utilitarian—polymers mostly, embellished with trim of stainless steel or aluminum—clean and pure and perfect. This felt like a cave from the days of old, over a millennium ago, when people purposely inhaled smoke to purposely addict themselves to deadly chemicals. It was another world altogether different, and that illustration was about to reveal itself in such a way that ignorance of it would no longer be permitted.

"Mr. President," the Chancellor started, "we are being served this evening with the help and effort of many good people. I sincerely hope that the cuisine meets to your liking. Tonight, we shall enjoy Caviar served with a wheat grain cracker, mushrooms with a cheese sauce made from the milk of goat, and that's just for starters. The main course will consist of pheasant under glass, served with shrimp scampi and tortellini alfredo. For beverages we have a lovely 2796 vintage Merlot from the vineyards of

Abernathy Squire, Britain Section, Sector Four—it's one of the best to come from that vineyard in decades, and I only have a few dozen bottles. I try never to insult my guests by serving anything younger than the century."

I was taken aback. I knew nothing of 'scampi' or 'Abernathy Squire' or even '2796.' I only knew that this is something out of a story, a centuries' old story of good and plenty, of embellishment, of opulence, and of great prosperity. Those times existed so far in the past for me and everyone in the Dome Confederation, that they were more myth than history. But now, to be sitting in its belly, was just, just—.

"Mr. Chancellor, I am really very honored to be the recipient of such opulence and spectacle. However, I must insist that we be told why we are here and what is to become of us. For all I know, if I were a suspicious person, the food could be poisoned or drugged, like the water, or worse—if I were a suspicious person. After all, drugging us with the water was not very conducive to negotiation openings, if that is your plan."

"My plan is to educate you, good sir." swiftly retorted the Chancellor.

"Educate me? I am need of education?" I was beginning to become frustrated with the riddle.

"Indeed. More than you could possibly imagine."

"I don't need to be educated, sir."

"You will see, Mr. President, that what you think you know, and what you do not know is a ratio greater in the hand than in your mind. Be mindful, good sir." You are in my domain and my world, a world you know absolutely nothing about. You would be wise to be patient and peaceful, for there is much reward for both our peoples, for the present, and for ages to come.

I began on the caviar and was taken away to a place in my mouth that had never been touched. The rest of the evening's eating was like a dream of absolute journey into a new world of flavor. I felt the guilt of one-hundred million emaciated souls barely surviving in the self-contained worlds that were their Domes. That was now about to change.

"Prepare yourself, Mr. President, to support your people and lead them to survival." With that comment I swallowed my last of the evening's food. I sat back and asked myself to be slow, open, and understanding. And the Chancellor told me about the reality of the world around me.

"I perceive my world, Mr. President, as one of great wealth and opportunity. These things however, have been largely untapped by my people. We are not represented by your government, and yours are not by mine."

"You keep saying your people. Where are these people? Where do they live? Surely nothing can survive for very long on the surface of this dying world."

The Chancellor laughed and replied, "We live everywhere, in everything. We eat the inedible, we cure the incurable, we believe in the unbelievable." The metaphors were confusing and dissimilar.

"I would appreciate a conversation in plain English." I shrugged and exhaled audibly.

"You think nothing of what I say? Do you insult me on purpose or are you just as blind as you appear? You say this world is dying, but, kind sir, when have you seen this world in its entirety?"

"Never. It is deadly most everywhere."

"And how long have your people believed that?"

"Generations. Our scientists confirmed our facts centuries ago, and they hold to that position today."

"So, you never thought in all those centuries that things might change out here—that our mother earth would heal from the torment that we, —humanity—have laid upon her? Ye have little faith, kind sir."

"Do you think me so naïve? Do you honestly believe me to be ignorant?"

"Of course not. I am attempting to illustrate to you, kind sir, that your perception is missing certain facts, and includes false premises, as I am sure my perception is missing facts about your culture." It was true that one's common perception with another is their reality. But it was also true that perceptions missing facts and based on false premises skew those perceptions beyond their common foundation. Hence, the missing facts to form commonalities between observers that define the truth have been the cause of debates, fights, conflicts and wars since the beginning of time. A third problem was that motivations placed behind agendas also skew perceptions. There is no pure perception when there exists an agenda and/or missing facts in one or more of the parties. Objective reality corrects all that corruption of perception.

"You misinterpret me, *kind sir*, in that I see far more than you perceive. Yes, while it is true that I know little of your government and the people you lead—that seem to exist right under our noses—," and that statement would turn out to be truer than I could imagine, "I know much of history and events that lead us to where we are today."

"Then by all means, tell me." And the Chancellor was eager to listen to all the historical nuances that lead to the destruction of the Golden Age and plunged the world into darkness. We spoke of the creators of the

Domes and the founding of the Dome Confederation. He was truly absorbing what I told him, and he acted as if he heard it all before.

"Let me show you something, kind sir."

Reilly broke, who had been listening intently to our conversation, "Mr. President, I insist I join you. This could be a trap." It was an utterance, barely audible to her and I.

"Reilly can join us?"

"Of course, kind sir. The gentle woman can come and see what I know."

With that we left the dining table, now emptied of food and garnishment, as the many servants were cleaning and working around us during the conversation. We were led through a hidden door which the Chancellor had opened by a remote control he pulled from his pocket. Through this he led us down a long hallway, which graded gradually downward. Lighting was sparse here—just enough light was thrown from the dim wall sconces that were spaced about every twenty feet or so—and just reflected enough light off the walls to illustrate their deep royal red color. We came to another door, of great and complex beauty, made of wood and stained a deep, rich brown color. The Chancellor opened the door by hand after speaking in his native tongue. The door opened, and we went forth.

Within the room was a control panel of sorts, and a monitor. The Chancellor showed Reilly and I what we already knew about our own history. There were moving pictures and computer models of events and statistics and news articles of the early years—all of which we had no knowledge existed. But more than that, he showed us the builders of the Domes, their plans and the true nature behind humanity's survival. We were startled to find out that part of the plans of the Domes that we were never shown, was the fact that beneath each Dome, was a survival complex of similar design, but below ground. Each complex could hold another million people, and neither group would have access or knowledge of the other. He explained that this was to ensure that at least one group or both would survive long enough to start the legacy of human civilization over again.

"We have both survived, kind sir, and *now* it is time to start over." The Chancellor looked me square in the eye and expected an answer. I was at a loss and in shock. I knew not what to say. Reilly took my hand and the world as we knew it fell away from our minds leaving only a blackened void of a future not known ahead for everyone involved.

The Chancellor continued, "I see your disbelief. I think I know your next question. You want to know how we found out about these plans before your people, and why we knew it was safe to go back outside."

"Partly."

"Well, kind sir, after generations had passed, the knowledge of the existence of the outside world was forgotten. After a while no one knew there was a sun, a surface, fresh air—everything. So, we, as all curious peoples do, began exploring and looking for more resources as the populations of our Places grew. We were always in contact with our other Places but didn't know where they were—I mean no one from one Place ever visited anyone from another. We had artificial lighting that mimicked the rhythms of night and day in a twenty-four-hour cycle. It was normal for us. There was nothing else.

"Like I said, we needed more raw materials and satisfactions of our own curiosity, so we began mining. First, down below the Places, then out, then up. Over decades our innocence was blasted away when we struck the surface. Broad daylight and fresh air, and blue skies were all brand new like the proverbial fish crawling out of the sea for the first time so many millions of years ago. But indeed, we were a fish out of water. Like your people we knew not how to survive in the open air. Many of us were killed by new bacteria and diseases for which we had no immunity. After our scientists caught up with the diseases, after a dozen generations, our population was only half of when we broke out. Our people split up and began colonizing areas of the surface. We found that some areas were deadly and inhospitable due to radiation poisoning, but most—most—were not. Most were green and lush and beautiful, and we no longer needed to look for more raw materials.

"We quickly learned to navigate across the seas. We discovered we lived on a globe after a short while. We explored, and mined, and found ruins of old civilizations long since dead—their knowledge once lost forever to the sands of eternity now rediscovered, for us, and for our children to wonder about.

"Our scientists worked feverishly to resurrect the old history of the End. We found that all the wonder that was new to our children in the ruins of that old civilization actually caused the End. They were a culture of many states and many languages—many different perceptions. Their rate of disagreement was so high that in many instances they murdered one another in order to gain the power to make their perception right. We found it nauseating. Then, we soon discovered that our own people, who by splitting off into their own settlements throughout this globe, were developing their own dialects, and perceptions. They were limited by and based upon only their own observations and not by the common knowledge that we shared when we were confined to the Places. The Places connected us. We all communicated together for the same purpose and governed ourselves with the greater good in mind. Now we were facing a period of darkness, of reduction of wisdom, of misperceptions and again, of violence. That will not happen! I can't let it.

"Shortly after this discovery, and our accompanying panic, we discovered this—your Dome—here in what you call Yucatan. There are no other Domes in the habitable regions of the globe."

"I can't believe that." I retorted. "I am the leader of one-hundred Domes across the planet, I myself am from the Dome in Washington, and since your people came from them, or below them, how could that be? You make no sense, *kind sir*."

"One hundred? I had no idea. I know of only four, all located here, and south of here."

"Again, Mr. Chancellor, where *is* here?" My anger was obvious, as I had been waiting patiently for the answer to that question all night long.

"We are right under your nose."

"What? Damn your metaphors! Answer the question!" I rose and angrily gestured towards the Chancellor. Reilly held me back by my left hand.

"Don't." She muttered.

"I will show you." He punched a few buttons on the control board and showed a map of the planet as he knew it. Highlighted were dots of lights that represented known human settlements under his leadership. "These are all outside, and above. All of them are out in the open. We haven't lived in the Places for at least five generations, which are those red lights—there." He gestured toward the monitor where the red lighted dots were, and relative to where I knew Yucatan Dome to be, we were in the southern continent, in the Great Mountains. From Yucatan Dome, from the top of the highest spires, three-thousand meters high, you can probably see them in the distance, on a clear day.

"How many years is that, Chancellor—those five generations?" I asked.

"Not too sure, kind sir. How long do your people live on average?"

"Eighty-five years."

"Really? That long?"

"Yeah."

"Let me see then," he paused, "looks like about one-hundred or so years on average. Our lifetimes are only thirty-five years. I myself am the oldest of my people, forty-seven, that is why I am Chancellor."

"Dear Lord!" Reilly interrupted, "Why do you suppose that could be?" asking both of us.

"I don't know, Reilly." I responded. "Maybe vitamin deficiency. We had to overcome that, centuries ago. Background radiation absorption is my guess. But we learned to supplement with organic minerals and designed and grew plants with specific minerals to compensate for that and most radiation-related illness. Maybe, maybe—sunlight! Yes, that must be it. Through centuries of living in your Places you said you had only artificial light, but no natural sunlight. Sunlight itself encourages the body to produce essential vitamins. Without it, life spans could certainly be shortened over time."

"You can prove this?"

"*You* should be able to."

"How?"

"Have your people began to live longer since your exodus out from your Places?"

"I don't know. It's been too early to tell. Perhaps in a few more generations, maybe."

"I can help you." With that we moved to another room in the vast labyrinth that was tiny in comparison, and suddenly and deliberately we were moving up. We both looked at each other, I looked at Reilly, she looked at me, and I looked back at the Chancellor. Then it dawned on all of us, and we said in unison, "There are ninety-six more Domes!"

"Chancellor," I asked, "You are sure you are only aware of four Places that your people all originated from?"

"Yes, kind sir, all located in this geographical vicinity."

"Well, if the plans you showed us are accurate, and the history you have—you have re-written for us is accurate, then there are ninety-six million people left under my Domes that have no idea that there is an outside world! Dear Lord, they might not have survived at all!" The room kept rising, as I felt myself get heavier and heavier. It was clear we were very deep originally and that we were moving at a very high rate of speed. Then, with all the Chancellor's goings on, I remembered that there were the million Confederation citizens of Yucatan Dome still missing! I had been so distracted that—.

"Chancellor, where are my people?"

"Safe."

"Are they hostages?"

"No. No, they are—are, my guests."

"Really? Guests? I'm sure. Where are my people, *kind sir*?" I did not trust him still. My perception of him was still that of an agenda embrangling my mind—his agenda. I was sure I had yet to meet the person behind his office. But perceptions are dangerous things. Any perception is based upon an equation that results in a measurable value of trust, which is reality; which of course only are the common perceptions of multiple observers. Perception equation of a person relative to oneself is as such: his actions divided by his agenda multiplied by the time of exposure to that man's actions minus the value of my actions divided by my agenda multiplied by the same value of time. The higher the value of time in the equation, the more reliable the value of the Perception equation's result is. If "A" represents the actions of the observed and "G" represents the agenda of the observed, and "C" represents the actions of the observer (me) and "N" represents the agenda of the observer (me), and "t" is the constant and unique value of true time experience between the two observers, then the equation is thus:

$$t\left\langle \frac{A}{G} - \frac{C}{N} \right\rangle = P$$

Anyone's agenda is a function of their upbringing, their physical and mental capabilities, their experiences, and most importantly, their language. Language plays the most important role in anyone's life, as an observer of things. It defines the logic base, the ability to communicate, and the projection to the cosmos of intent. Language can be in any form—vocal, gestured, active, psychic, written—anything that can be used to communicate to another observer is considered language. To place a value here, the more research about a person's history, upbringing, life choices and psychological state, will produce the most accurate agenda value.

If the values of each variable in the Perception equation have a value from zero to ten, where ten is the one-hundred percent influential on the observer, and zero is zero percent influential on the observer, then a person's perception of the perception of another can be measured concretely. The agenda value of any observer can never be zero. Otherwise, the equation results in an undefined term of a value divided by zero (perhaps Christ was such a person). The Chancellor's actions have been almost completely motivated by his agenda at this point in my conversations with him, so his agenda value I would place at eight or nine. Suppose its value is eight. Therefore, his action value can be no other number but two, as there can be no value higher than ten, because ten represents one-hundred percent of an observer's influence on his actions. So, the overall subjective judgment of any person relative to us, the observer, is a subjective assessment of that observer of a combination of the two values of actions and agenda.

Time is measured in pure time—which is to say that it's in seconds of absolute experience, which is measured in seconds of common experience. The two values, for the Chancellor and myself, must be the same. If the equation were to be applied to Reilly, then her value of time may be different than mine, but it will still be an equal number to the Chancellor's. The Chancellor's value of time, relative to both myself and Reilly, will be two different values. Hence, any one observer will always have a unique value of time in the equation for all other observers in their experience. Time itself is measured in seconds of mutual experience. The mutual experience shared between the Chancellor and myself in terms of time has been a little over seven hours, seven hours ten minutes which translates into twenty-five thousand eight-hundred seconds of mutual experience. If time of common experience is zero, then the overall Perception value will be zero.

However, one can learn about historical facts surrounding an individual, his actions, and his agenda. But that will always be through the perception of a third-party interpretation, no matter how accurate that interpretation. This causes a breakdown of reliability in the resulting Perception value. With the third party involved, the previous equation would have to include the actions and agenda values of the third party in question, thus:

$$t\left(\frac{A}{G}-\frac{A_1}{G_1}-\frac{C}{N}\right)=P$$

As more and more interpretations stand between the observer and the common experience, the more subtracted fractions must be included to get the observer's Perception value. The time shared, say, between the author of a book, or a producer of a documentary, is the time measured of common experience between the intermediate observers communicating the information. Therefore, education is such the powerful force in the cosmos. Common experience can be stored, communicated, and shared at any time, not just the instant of occurrence. To maintain historical accuracy is the most important endeavor for us to do. Second only to the projection of love to others, knowledge is the most powerful force in the cosmos.

My agenda value through this meeting so far has been significantly smaller than the Chancellor's. My agenda includes securing the safety of my missing people, our own safety, and keeping my guard up to a strange person with new and different ideas. I place my "N" value at four. Meanwhile, my "C" value, then, must be a six to make one-hundred percent influence on my actions.

Applying these values to the formula yields a Perception value of negative thirty-two thousand two-hundred and fifty. The Perception value is always indicative of the level of trust one can place in the intent of the other. A negative value indicates that trust must be built to reach a consensus, to find the common perceptions to define each other's reality, while a positive value indicates that trust is high and the common perceptions between the two have reached a high level of reality. A husband and wife married for twenty years will have a Perception value in the billions to the positive, unless it is revealed that one or both have been withholding information from one another, which increases the agenda value, thus decreasing the perception value and throwing it back into the negative. The goal in any negotiation or relationship or test of reality is to achieve a Perception value that is positive.

Judging another's agenda value is a highly subjective matter. I as the calculator of the equation can place an agenda value on the Chancellor far higher than he may place on himself. Therefore, our two equations may yield a very different result. Hence, before attempting to work towards a positive value, the two parties must agree on a starting value. That requires communication, and that is why language, and culture, and all those other things I mentioned before that encompass an observer's actions are so important. To calculate, one must communicate. Further, the equation fails when information is withheld by one or both observers. Consequently, honesty is critical to the success of any negotiation. Agenda inhibits honesty, and hence the accuracy of the Perception value. Therefore, deception is absolute destruction of perception. One should never deceive (or omit, which is the absence of perception) and greatly skews the result.

I turned to the Chancellor and on a risk told him what I thought he wanted to do about the other ninety-six Places. "You want to crack all of the Domes, don't you?"

"Yes. That's right. It's the only way, kind sir."

"Then what? After that how do we get to the others below? You yourself showed us that there was no access from one Dome to the Place below. What is it you are not telling me? If you want the cooperation of—if you want *my* cooperation, *kind sir*, you must trust me."

He turned to me and said, "Trust, Mr. President, is something I know little about. I am used to having my way. I am very used to that."

"Well you will have to get *un*-used to it, because the only way we are going to resurrect humanity is together, as partners, as responsible leaders, and as caretakers of our world."

"Yes. Yes–," a long pause and, "Yes! We shall use our digging techniques and teach all your people the ways and means to reach my people below. I wonder how different they will be, if they are even alive, from the world I know as my own.

"That, *kind sir*, will be for both of us to discover, together."

With that the door re-opened again revealing the great outside as the sunlight of the rising (or setting) sun (I could not tell which then, time being relative and local, and all) warmly caressed my face and blinded my eyes. As my eyes adjusted to the brightness I saw in front of me a vast crowd of people–my people–the missing people from Yucatan Dome. They turned, looked and in unison, began cheering and reveling at the wonderful discovery that befell them–that the air outside could be breathed! It was pure, good, and fresh! Their–and our–time of imprisonment was over. It was finally, over!

The Chancellor again turned to me and muttered over the volume of the crowd, "We must give them all a gift, Mr. President."

"A gift?"

"Yes. We must lead them. We must give the human race the chance it needs to do it all over again but do it right this time. Now we must give them a document—a Constitution—that acknowledges our mistakes as a species, acknowledges our ancestors' mistakes and failings for the benefit of earth—Terra Firma—and that acknowledges every voice of every observer that will ever live here in the wonderful, vast planet we have been given, and beyond."

"Beyond?"

"Yes, of course! There are so many worlds to call home and we can and should go forth and multiply! It will ensure our survival, beyond the self, beyond the nation, but for the whole of humanity."

I saw the light of it. A bright, blinding, radiant light in my mind filled me in a way I hadn't felt before. "Then we have much work to do, Chancellor. When shall we begin?"

He said and smiled at me, "Mr. President, we already have."

And that was the beginning of the New Age of humankind. Vast exploration and colonization of the many Places began and then accelerated. Wherever humanity went, something would be brought with them. The Chancellor and I tirelessly worked on what has become the cornerstone of human civilization while all the Domes and all of the Places were liberated one by one. Communications between all peoples were set up with our combined existing technology and, one by one, the Citizens' Constitution of Terra Firma was read by millions, and then ratified by those millions. The responsibility we all share and acknowledge are reflected in its pages, and even though it is a document that every person has read over and over again within the past forty years, I shall provide it here, in *these* pages, for all those who care to listen—who feel responsible, who are the caretakers of all of us, and of mother earth—Terra Firma—the beloved, the Gift.

~

Citizens' Constitution of Terra Firma

We the Citizens of Terra Firma, hereby decree that a Democratic Representative Government exist to establish justice, end tyranny, provide for the common defense, maintain the public order, to establish and uphold the basic unalienable rights and responsibilities of all Citizens, do hereby acknowledge the responsibility we place upon ourselves, to maintain the health and welfare of the Ecosystem of the Planet Earth, and all worlds, to preserve the birthplace of our origins in order to ensure our preservation, do ordain and establish this Constitution for the Citizens of Terra Firma.

Article I **Representative Districts**

1. There shall exist **Representation by Population** for every 10,000 - 29,999 Citizens in habitation of a **Volume** containing that number. Two **Representatives** will be elected by the originating population from within their **Volume**. Each **Representative** will be chosen by a popular vote of which the majority winner will be then the **Majority Representative** and the next highest in popularity will be then the **Minority Representative**. All other candidates will not be counted.

A. In the event of the population of a **Volume** reaches 19,999 Citizens in habitation therein, the next 10,000 Citizens that arise in habitation above and beyond the original 19,999 Citizens shall form the next, new **Volume.**
B. In the event of the population of an existing **Volume** declines below 10,000 Citizens, that Volume shall be dissolved, and its population be absorbed into **Volumes** whose population is less than 29,999 Citizens.

Section 1 **Representative Qualifications/Elections and Terms**

1. The eligibility of Representatives shall be contingent upon their completion of their thirtieth year of life, and minimum educational requirements that shall include but not be limited to mathematics, logic, reason, economics, communication, debate, and psychology.
2. Neither Race, color, creed, sex, sexual orientation, financial status, physical ability, method of communication, nor veteran status will restrict the nomination, election, or rights to serve of any citizen seeking public office of any kind.
    a. All Candidates for Representative shall be afforded equal opportunity to communicate their opinions to voting Citizens without restriction due to personal physical, financial, and/or communicational limitations.
3. Eligible Representative candidates must have voted in the previous 3 election sessions.
4. In the event of the death of a Majority Representative, the Minority Representative shall act as Majority Representative (and no Minority Representative shall exist) until such time as an emergency election can be held in the Volume for Majority Representative and Minority Representative.
5. Representatives will be expected to govern above all else personal or professional so that no conflict of interest shall exist within them.
6. Election sessions will occur every five years.

7. There shall exist no political parties or organizations that restrict the rights of any one Citizen to pursue any public office in any way.
8. Representatives elected to higher offices within this Constitution shall be replaced by a special election of the Citizens from within the Volume from which the vacant Representative was elected.
9. There shall be no appointing of Representatives.

2. Upon election, Representatives elected from within each Volume will be given to the **House of Representatives** for their **Sector**. A **Sector** will consist of no greater than one hundred twenty-five Volumes in a contiguous group.

A. This Constitution recognizes that opinions can differ within one person about any one topic. (Ergo: There is agreement with some parts of a bill, but disagreement with other parts.)

1. Both Majority and Minority Representatives will cast 4 votes, or Ballots, on any one bill (Example: Referendum 17: Tom Smith votes 3 = YES / 1 = NO). Specificity shall not be required.
2. Votes can be cast as "**yes**," "**no**," or "**no commitment**" when so desired on any one bill.
3. Bills shall be submitted to the Supreme Council with a 60% majority affirmative vote on the bill.
4. Only the **House of Representatives** can submit Bills to the Supreme Council (not related to the National Budget).
5. All submitted Bills shall be presented and debated equally and fairly, with no discrimination of source, in the order in which they are presented. There shall be no filibustering ever, in any way used in the process of governing or making laws.
10. **Emergency Sessions** of a House of Representatives can be declared and rescinded by the **House of Representatives** at any time, for any reason, by a simple majority vote.
    a. The Chancellor can, if in the instance of abuse of this entitlement by the House(s) of Representatives, rescind any Declaration of Emergency.

11. There shall be no Lobby for special interests in any Houses of Representatives, in the Supreme Council or in the office of the Chancellor.
12. Only the Houses of Representatives, Supreme Council, and the Chancellor will prioritize legislation.

Article II - **Citizen Groups**

1. All eligible voting Citizens shall be afforded the opportunity to participate in a **Citizen Group** by which **Bills can be created and proposed** to their Volume Majority and Volume Minority Representatives.

   A. No Citizen Group will be greater than one hundred-sixty Citizens, and no less than Eighty Citizens.

   B. No Citizen Group as an entity, nor any individual Citizen, can turn away, shun, punish, ignore, segregate or otherwise adversely impact any Citizen of voting age wishing to participate and/or for any opinion communicated at any time by that Citizen in any Citizen Group regardless of sex, sexual orientation, creed, color, race, method of communication, religion, veteran status, or physical ability; and they will participate in all proceedings as equal partners with all others.

      1. Loyalty to any one Citizen Group, or groups of Citizen Groups, shall not be observed or displayed either publicly or privately by any one or groups of Citizens nor shall coats of arms, flags, colors, or icons be displayed or inferred to represent any Citizen Group at any time. We do ordain this for the free flow of ideas and opinions within any Citizen Group or groups of Citizen Groups.
      2. Citizens will not be restricted to participate in only one Citizen Group if they so choose, provided the number of Citizens within the Citizens Group does not exceed one hundred-sixty.
         a. A Citizen's right to belong to one Citizens Group outweighs another Citizen's right to belong to multiple Citizens Groups.

C. All Citizen Groups from within the Volume, from time to time, shall collaborate in the creation of **Joint Bill proposals**.
   1. All **Joint Bill proposals** will be ratified within all the proposing Citizen Groups by a sixty-five percent majority vote prior to their passing to the Volume Majority and Volume Minority Representatives.

D. Bills deemed not eligible for submission to the Volume House of Representatives for vote by the Volume Majority and Volume Minority Representatives shall be responded back to the originating Citizen Group in the form of an **Official Descending Opinion** which will detail the truthful reasons for refusal within six months from the date of submission to the Volume Majority and/or Volume Minority Representative without deception, omission, manipulation or any means that distorts the reasoning of the Opinion.

Article III **Executive - Supreme Council/Chancellor**

1. Each Sector House of Representatives will nominate one serving Representative that will serve their term as Representative as a **Supreme Council President**, if elected by the Sector's House of Representatives by a simple majority vote.
2. The Supreme Council can have any number of **Supreme Council Presidents**, provided that each Supreme Council President represents a different Sector.

Section 1 **Powers of the Supreme Council**

A. The Supreme Council will receive Bills from all the Sector Houses of Representatives and have the power to make Laws by **"enacting" Bills into Laws**. This is done by a simple majority vote of the Supreme Council. All other Declarations will be by a simple majority vote of the Supreme Council Presidents.

B. Each Supreme Council President will cast only one vote.

C. Only the Supreme Council can declare War.

D. The Supreme Council must ratify all foreign policy agreements made by the Chancellor by a simple majority vote.
E. Only the Supreme Council can declare an Emergency.
F. The Supreme Council cannot make laws without a formally submitted Bill from either the Houses of Representatives or the Chancellor.
G. Only the Supreme Council can ratify Supreme Court Justice Nominees into the Supreme Court, through a simple majority vote.
H. Only the Supreme Council can pass clemency of crimes to any Citizen Associate.

Section 2 **Election of Chancellor**

A. Supreme Council Presidents can run for the position of Chancellor, which will be elected through a Citizen-wide Election Session, through a simple majority vote of the total population, once every five years.
    1. In the event of the existence of only one Sector, the Supreme Council (of one President) will also be Chancellor.
    2. Citizens choosing not to participate in voting will forfeit debate rights for the period of one year directly following the election.

Section 3. **Powers of Chancellor**

A. Only the Chancellor will have power over the military as the Commander in Chief.
    1. The military will provide for the defense of the territory protected by this Constitution by any aggressive force.
    2. The military will provide for the defense against all possible Global Extinction Events.
    3. The military will provide for the defense of innocent Citizens against committers all criminal behaviors.
    4. The military will not discriminate against any member based on any issue, other than age, health and physical and/or mental capability.

5. No one unit of the military shall contain any larger than ten percent of its Human fighting force from any one Volume or Sector.

B. Only the Chancellor will have the power to negotiate foreign policy with other Governmental Bodies.
C. Only the Chancellor will have the power to nominate Supreme Court Justices.
    1. Justices will be named from previous members of the Supreme Council and/or Chancellors that are no longer serving as Supreme Council President or Chancellor but have been out of office no more than two election sessions (twelve years).
    2. In the event that no previous Chancellors and/or Supreme Council members are in existence, Justices will be nominated by the current Chancellor from current Supreme Council Presidents of the Supreme Council.
D. Only the Chancellor will have the power to divert funds in times of Emergency.
E. The Chancellor will have full Ruling Power in times of Emergency, with full ability to make Laws that apply only to the Resolution of an Emergency, without consent of the House of Representatives and/or the Supreme Council and will be effective for a maximum period of one month and will never be used to usurp the authority of this Constitution or governing bodies defined herein.
F. The Chancellor will on a yearly basis publicly address the State of Terra Firma with the Citizens.
G. The Chancellor is responsible for creating and presenting a balanced budget to the Supreme Council every year. Budgets submitted by the Chancellor are treated as and do become Bills in the Supreme Council but take priority over all others, and is an exception to the in order by clause.
H. The Chancellor may set aside any lands, for the purpose of preserving their natural state for future generations, at any time and in any location and to improve infrastructure needs as required by the Nation as a whole, and for its purposeful direct benefit.

Section 4 **Emergencies**

A. Emergencies consist of Invasion by a foreign group of beings against Terra Firma, Terrorist Action against Terra Firma, Natural Disaster; Technological Disaster; Civil War and/or overwhelming Civil Disturbance; Biological Disaster; and all possible Global Extinction Events.
B. Emergencies can be specific to a region of a Volume, Volume, Sector, Body, Planet, or all of Terra Firma and thereby applicable to such.

Article IV **Judicial**

1. All Defendants shall have the right to a trial by a jury of peers, that will be selected by agreement between the Experts of Law representing the Plaintiff and Defendant, and will be no less than fifteen members who will decide guilt or innocence by no less than a twelve to three majority, beyond a reasonable doubt, and will begin within a reasonable time from the date of arrest, not to exceed one year.
    A. Defendants shall not be tried on more than one occasion for any one event regardless of the number of accusations relating to that event.
    B. All evidence in all cases tried in all courts shall be heard in totality.
    C. Financial and Criminal consequences are deemed equivalent and as such are considered double jeopardy when pursued together. There shall be pursued only one course of punishment for any violation of law.
    D. There will be no recourse of any kind against an individual (or group of individuals) who have been found to be not guilty of an accusation through the due process of law unless new evidence of guilt is produced; a new trial would be warranted for the Event previously tried.
        1. In this instance, the jury consisting of the same members as the original jury for the Event previously tried shall hear all previous evidence before hearing the new evidence.
        2. In the event that jury members are not in existence or otherwise unavailable, jury selection will occur to fill the missing juror, under the same guidelines as stated herein (*see Article IV, Section 1*).

E. No fear of harm whether it is physical, psychological, or financial, perceived or otherwise, shall be invoked or reckoned upon any such individual who has been found to be not guilty of an accusation.
    1. No entity or employer will terminate gainful employment based on accusations in a court proceeding until such time as establishment of guilt is concluded and the defendant has been found guilty and a punishment has been sentenced.

F. Defendants found guilty of an accusation, have the right to appeal to the next highest court (Sector Court and/or Supreme Court).

G. All defendants are entitled to representation by an Expert of Law at no financial burden to that defendant who will provide the most thorough and enthusiastic defense to the best of their abilities at all times.

H. All defendants shall not be forced to bear witness against one's self or incriminate one's self in a crime.

I. Equal numbers of Experts of Law shall represent plaintiffs and defendants.

J. Defendants proven guilty of any crime forfeit their Citizenship, and thereby protection under this Constitution, except for the following as Citizen Associates:
    1. A Citizen Associate will have the right to Representation by an Expert of Law who will be responsible for the proving of the Citizen Associate's innocence and bringing forth any and all appeals.
    2. The Citizen Associate's Expert of Law shall act as Citizen on their behalf and will exercise any and all rights under this Constitution as the advocate of the Citizen Associate
    3. Citizen Associates shall not be subject to physical, mental, psychological, or spiritual abuse, and/or punishment or treatment that is not as a part of the sentence imposed on them as payment for the crimes they have committed.
    4. Citizen Associates shall not be given work without the due compensation of the fair minimum wage for any Citizen, as stated by law, or economic equilibrium.

5. Citizen Associates shall not be subject to cruel or unusual punishments, but will be subject to punishment that will be, by its nature, unpleasant and unrewarding.
6. Citizen Associates that are later to be proven innocent of the crime for which they are convicted, are entitled to compensation from the government for their unlawful punishment, relative to the length of time or severity of their sentence.

K. Defendants only can make appeals to higher courts.

2. One court will exist in each Volume to hear and judge the guilt or innocence of Citizens accused of committing acts that violate laws passed by the Supreme Council and that are contained herein.

    A. Volume Court Judges will be elected by the Citizens of the Volume and will be held to the same requirements, standards, and qualifications as Representatives.

3. One Court will exist in each Sector to hear and judge the reasonability of appeals of Defendants of Volume court's decisions by accused Defendants.

    A. Sector Court judges will be elected by the House of Representatives from serving Volume Court judges within the Sector by a simple majority vote.
    B. Volume court vacancies will be filled through a simple majority vote of the House of Representatives of serving Representatives.
    C. Sector Courts may at any time reject any appeal due to lack of evidence of support for the appeal.

4. The Supreme Court will consist of a panel of Judges of fifteen who will hear appeals brought forth from accused Defendants found guilty of crimes from Sector Courts and to address primarily cases that deal with the Constitutionality of laws passed by the Supreme Council and has the power to declare such laws as Unconstitutional and thereby revoking said laws.

A. Only the Supreme Court can try a Representative, Supreme Council President, Chancellor, or Judge, accused of a crime.
   1. The Supreme Council will be responsible for the trying of a Supreme Court Judge accused of a crime, or remove another judge in any court, including the Supreme Court, for infirmity or unfitness for duty.

B. Any Holder of Office found guilty of a crime after both appeals have been heard (or denied) shall be removed from office upon immediate action. The guilty will have no recourse to run for office of any kind, nor vote in any election session until proof of innocence is established through due judicial process.

Article V **Public Recompense**

1. If at any time, a member of elected office falls out of favor with the Citizens within the Volume or Sector electing them, a **Public Election of Standing** can be held at any time within that Volume or Sector.
   A. By a two-thirds majority, the Election of Standing is empowered to remove from office any holder thereof.
   B. Removal from office will not affect past actions by the holder of the office in the capacity of the office that was held.
2. If at any time any member of the Supreme Council and/or Chancellor and/or Supreme Court Judge falls out of favor with the people of the Planet, a Public Election of Standing can be held at any time.
   A. By a two-thirds majority the election is empowered to remove them from office.
   B. Removal from office will not affect past actions by the holder of the office in the capacity of the office that was held.
3. If at any time a law passes through the Supreme Council that falls out of favor with the Citizens of the Planet, a public Election of Law can be held at any time.
   A. By a two-thirds majority the election is empowered to Veto said Law.
   B. The overturning of a Law will reverse past actions effected by that Law.
4. If at any time a declaration of emergency falls out of favor with the Citizens of the Volume, Sector, or Planet, a public Election of Declaration can be held at any time.

   A. By a two-thirds majority the election is empowered to remove them from office.
5. By a simple majority popular vote in the Volume or Sector, an Election of Standing, an Election of Law, or Election of Emergency can be called.

Article V **Ministry of Resources**

1. The House of Representatives for each Sector will elect a Majority Representative to the Ministry of Resources.
2. Responsibilities:
   A. To manage Preserved Regions which will be set aside as wild and natural areas that will be no less than one-third the surface (not to include the verticality of said Region) of the Planet (land and ocean) to maintain the Natural Balance of the Ecosystem, of which half will be rain forest and other oxygen-producing areas.
      1. Trespassing on these regions will not be tolerated, except for purposes of scientific exploration and the apprehension of criminals or criminal suspects.
      2. Great care shall be taken as to not damage, destroy, or otherwise injure or disrupt the environment within Preserved Regions.
      3. Preserved Regions will be no less than ten thousand acres and/or equivalent square nautical miles individually.
         a. The vertical volume limits of these Regions will be one hundred miles in altitude from Sea Level and one hundred miles in depth from Sea level.
         b. Priority resides in the creation of continuous stretches of Preserved Regions being created before separated minimal Regions.
         c. Preserved Regions will always include no less than one half of their required area in land.
   B. To explore in the Planet and on any other planet (or body) in conjunction with any existing private industry never to be less than half of the contribution, possible ways and means to extract any and all useful resources to provide for the betterment of existence for all Citizens of the Planet.
   C. To manage the recycling of existing discarded consumer goods for the usable raw materials contained therein for the purpose of reusing their existence as themselves additional sources of the raw material contained therein.

D. To manage the collection, recycling, and/or sanitary destruction and/or sanitary elimination of all consumer waste.
    1. Consumer waste will include, but is not limited to, biological, industrial, nuclear, corporate and private waste.

E. To provide for the expansion of life from the Planet to other locations, anywhere, in conjunction with any existing private industry never to be less than half of the contribution.

F. To maintain an accelerated level of scientific research in all fields of expertise to expand and enrich the existence of all Citizens in conjunction with any existing private industry never to be less than half of the contribution.

G. To maintain at all times a free and unhindered, private Postal System that shall, by obligation, be available to all Citizens and shall be technologically current with the accepted venue of the day.

Article VI **Ministry of Education**

1. The Ministry of Education shall provide for the most advanced educational level possible for all Citizens in conjunction with any existing private industry, never to be less than half of the physical or financial contribution in order to maintain such levels.
2. All Citizens shall be duty bound to engage in their own education at similar levels with all others as ability permits.
3. The Ministry of Education shall protect, preserve all objects and structures of antiquity and cultural value.
    A. No Citizen shall damage, destroy or otherwise deface any object or structure of antiquity.

Article VII **Ministry of Communications**

1. All information relating to current events, issues and happenings, which would warrant legislation in any way, are to be communicated by the Press to the Citizens, the Houses of Representatives, the Supreme Council, and the Chancellor.
    A. The primary responsibility of the press will be to communicate all occurrences to the Citizens, the Houses of Representatives, the Supreme Council, and the Chancellor.

B. The Press shall not engage in the willful communication of misleading, misinterpreting, exaggerating, falsifying and or otherwise untrue information for any reason.
C. The Press will report all that is reportable without the withholding of any information, without violating any and all rights to privacy of any and all Citizens, unless in the investigation of a warranted crime as restricted by this Constitution.
D. The Press will not engage in acts in the name of information gathering that will physically endanger any Citizen or group of Citizens.
E. The Press will report any and all information that is reported to the Houses of Representatives, Supreme Council, and Chancellor, to all Citizens as promptly and completely as possible.
F. The press shall not in any way construct information that is false, misleading, uninformed, omitted, contrived, derived, or imagined that is not in direct correlation to exact facts in evidence.
G. The press shall not contribute to rioting or the inciting of rioting in any way.

Article VIII **Employer Compliance**

1. Under any circumstances is it lawful for an Employer to restrict the rights of any Citizen that are stated within this document.
2. Punishment for such action by any Employer against any Citizen will be the equivalent monetary compensation for that Citizen of One Hundred Thousand ounces of 24K Gold of its value on January 1st of 2000.
3. Employers doing business within the jurisdiction of this Constitution are subject to the limits, rules, and protection as a Citizen of Terra Firma under this Constitution.
4. Employers shall not engage in the production of items or engage in the marketing of products that are proven physically or mentally unhealthy to Citizens, addictive, or in any way against the scientific level of knowledge and recommendation of the day, in conjunction with the established medical profession of the day.
5. Any formal Employer workday shall not be required to be greater than (but not restricted to) six consecutive waking hours and shall not be longer than six consecutive working days for any one Citizen who has not been elected to Representative office.

6. Every seventh day will be a day of rest for all Citizens who have not been elected to Representative office.
7. Employers shall allow and make available four working shifts of six hours available for the maximum number of Citizens economically allowable.

Article IX **Amendments**

1. Amendments to this Constitution will be brought forth from the Houses of Representatives by a simple majority vote and then will be passed to the Supreme Council, where by a simple majority vote, will be brought forth to a Citizen Amendment Ratification Vote where by a two-thirds majority vote of all eligible voting Citizens.

For one and all, do we the undersigned, ordain and accept the responsibilities placed upon ourselves by the acceptance of this Constitution to govern, direct, and embark within our Society as Human Brethren, the causes to live, grow and flourish, as the Caretakers of Ourselves, our Planet of Origin and, anywhere we shall live.

VI

Song

I lose no logic to you for I am the only next step to take.

December 18, 2034. 94:31am(#%$H19); Saturn System, Titan, Ergon Vinculum Mare Confederation.

So many tubes...Haze...Orange Haze...Rings...Saturn. Neptune? Why Neptune? Triton. Blackening. Fading... Life is indeed the culmination of a series of decisions (or indecisions) that a person makes every single day. These steps, open doors to pass through that would otherwise never be able to be opened, if a certain decision is made. The decisions shape the cosmos of all observers, their lives, their worlds, and their contributions.

My nightmare was culminating in a final judicious event that would once and for all prove to the tormenting soul of my nemesis that she was no longer, or never was, my master—that I was the master of all things, and her decision to disprove me, influenced and opened a door to me that led to our mutual shutting of other doors. This final event would forever change her, and myself, and I would no longer be able to be victimized by her anymore. In a sense, there are no victims, ever. Events that lead to the premature demise of a person are all due to decisions made by that person. Even something as awful as a terrorist attack on thousands of innocent people was created by the decisions of those people to go to work that day, to get a job in that firm, to go to school to specialize in that field of work, to make lots of money, to be successful, to contribute to society, whatever it is, for every event, there are an infinite number of decisions that lead to it.

I never knew a soul to be so odd, so stoic, so cold, and yet had the ability to see great detail, at the expense of the big picture—the very big picture. When the "big picture" was brought up in conversation, it was me who was accused of not seeing it. Imagine, to be able to observe events so far removed from their source, that those close to its source feel they can accuse me of not seeing what is in my mind as small a detail as any other and call it the 'big picture.' She tormented me in this manner, and in the manner of frustration leading to my—this—reaction. I am greater than all her expectations put together, and to her, that was the end of this thing. For me however, I needed to prove beyond all else that I was as wise and as vital as I felt, and for others to see that value, was paramount to my success in the battle.

She knows exactly what she does, in the context of her own cosmos, but to her, the cosmos consists of a few dozen people—family and friends—scattered throughout the eastern seaboard. For me, however, my cosmos is vast as vast can be—quadrillions of observers in an almost infinite cosmos, from the heart of a black hole to the muon filled end state of a cosmos run down like a dying watch. I could see the future, the past, the instantaneous present, all directions, infinite dimensions upon dimensions, and the One, who exists in all places at all times, our Lord, Savior and Creator. Strangely enough however, there exists the most basic observation that everything truly only exists in the instant of time that we, as observers through the instant, perceive as the "present." It is difficult for most to grasp this concept intellectually. Regular folks for certain but educated folks and all others in higher educational circles can see and touch upon this fact, but rarely approach its explanation.

Its explanation includes memory, and sentience created by memory of observers of a cosmos that truly only exists in three dimensions. The fourth dimension, of time, is an illusion created by our own memories—the biologically recorded events of instantaneous 'presence' from before the current one. Even the act of typing one letter on this page is infinitely longer than the instant of time the entire cosmos exists in. Our error as observers of our cosmos is that we misperceive our memory and our ability to mentally predict events as "time." Beyond that, the accumulation of instantaneous snapshots of those instances of time—our memory—we also perceive as "action," and "motion"—all in all, change of any kind. This includes change in position, change in the weather, change in financial status, and change in mood. It includes much more. It is the cosmos's way of validating our own existence, so that we may validate the existence of the cosmos.

We perceive the cosmos around us, therefore it exists. With no observer to perceive the cosmos, the cosmos does not—cannot—exist. This was my "big picture." She—my tormentor—was but a muon among quadrillions of muon-latent cold, dark, empty space, amongst quadrillions of perceptions, amongst an infinite imagination, amongst all of the imaginations of all the observers within the very same cosmos. She, I concluded, was a tormenting soul because of her own insecurities in her own perceptions of the cosmos. These perceptions created a cosmos within her life that was too small to fulfill her detailed and organized mind. She did not, however, pick up on the fact that her attention to the details created their own limitations in the way she perceived that cosmos. One begets the other. I was never so engrossed with the subject in my nightmare before. But the actions, and inaction, on her behalf relative to me were so inadequate and trivial, that one could only draw those conclusions.

Or she simply cared so much about her own perception, that mine did not matter—carried no, or little, weight—in hers.

So, I turned to the one thing that I could most diligently express myself with. It was the one thing that could account for the complexities and uniqueness of the human perception of time. And it was the one thing that could create what I considered beauty. That one thing was music. I used it in order to counteract the most destructive of criticisms coming from the tormenting soul. Now, since the cosmos itself exists only in an instant of what we perceive as "time," the gift we have of sentience, based upon the retention of memory of previous events, allows music itself to exist. For, what is music but our ability to hear or play a note or a chord, and relate that note or chord to another one in mathematical ratios relative to each other? This all can happen because we, as sentient beings, have the ability to remember the time when a note was played, then play a second note in relationship to the first. Then a third in relationship to the second could be played, and so forth and so on.

Then we can play those notes in varying intervals of 'time' in order to create something that creates a biological response in our brains that releases endorphins, invokes an emotional response, and hence provides pleasure to the listener, or the player. It is a microcosm of relative perceptions between a creator and an audience of music. This is all a microcosm of Creation itself, the very point, the truth, and the wonder of it all. The act of creation is the divine act within all of us that have been blessed in each of us as a Gift from our Creator. The limitations of our perceptions do not do the truth of infinite information justice, that is the cosmos, between the beginning and the end, the alpha and the omega, as the divine truth, and objective reality that we peer through the tiniest, infinitesimally small of keyholes.

With that act in my nightmare, I know I could defeat the tormenting soul at her own game, and show her, and all others who wish to learn, that perception is nothing more than the individual response of an observer to a collection of notes played in our Creator's mind. Every perception is unique to every observer, and since the Creator is also an observer, with no observer, there can be no Creator of the Creator. Hence, the Creator is in our image as well as we are in His. But because He is that who Creates apart from the flow of time, His Creation is the validation of His existence. I thought of all this in my half-awake state before waking up fully, through the tunnel of light, and then I was in my new world.

I saw several people before me, and all was brightly lit and white. They were human, and I knew the exact time and date, at the instant of its happening, but I had no memory of the previous measurements of those.

One of the men said to another, "Tom, place these calculations into the computer and see where it takes them."

Excitedly, Tom responded, "Yes doctor Brennan." As Tom was entering in the information, he asked the doctor, "So how close do you think we are?"

"I'm not quite sure, son. I would like to believe that these formulas will be what the most sophisticated computer on the planet needs, and can handle, to solve the mystery. After all, in 2197 you'd think we could figure all this out."

"I see, doctor."

Tom had interned with Dr. Michael Brennan, child prodigy and now excommunicated eccentric researcher, for a little under two years. He was nearing twenty-six and still hadn't figured out what his focus should be, his interests never fully aligning with the accepted research paths in the field and never seeming to gain support in the academic community for many of his relatively outlandish, and unsubstantiated ideas—

unsubstantiated relative to other researchers. That is why he chose to intern with Brennan, his mind and his own were very similar: quirky, imaginative, and unbounded. He finished entering the formulas and calculations into the computer. At that moment, I began to perceive things that I had not before—truths and ideas and realities so vast that I struggled to account for every single one. They too, for me, were *unbounded.* I began to slow my thoughts, in reaction to Tom's inputs. I felt as if the entire cosmos was opening inside my mind. And I soon found out that it was, outside of it as well.

As if being locked into a stream of pure knowledge, Tom's formulas were based on Dr. Brennan's paper that won him nothing but criticism, public humiliation and excommunication from his peers. It was his ideas that the research community refused to accept on any level simply because they were too far removed from the current thinking: too many steps forward from the stationary point of safe Groupthink for anyone to risk their careers and reputations on. Dr. Brennan, the once great prodigy, now insanely mad scientist. A man. And one to be clearly avoided lest everyone became contaminated by his poison thoughts.

His ideas were simple really, that started with Special Relativity and the idea that Time is Local and relative. Therefore, he surmised in a thought experiment, the physics describing the dimensions time interacts with are also local, and relative. He also described how in physics equations that describe the universe, they are inexorably trapped in the dimensional mode for which they are perceived, (i.e., they cannot describe higher dimensions in space or time because they run into infinity values, such as in gravitation time and information in a black hole).

Infinities (∞) in spatial descriptive equations represented dimensional boundaries indicating a change of vector in the infinity state whereby the math describing paths of energy moves into descriptivism relative to the next nearest dimensional order and turns out to be the mathematical representation of said dimensional transition. Thus, when current physics equations uncover infinities in their results and cannot be simplified further, they are describing higher or lower dimensions in the cosmos that are observed relative to the three-dimensional spatial dimension within which we exist and that our physics describes mathematically from a perspective that is ontologically due to the minds perceiving that dimension in describing it. And that they can ultimately be solved trigonometrically.

For example, he described, there is a point that exists, objectively, and as its own dimension. It, itself, does not experience any direction we can perceive, like forward, backward, right, or left. It exists in its own dimension, as itself. What actions can it take? None, relative to us. It cannot spin, wiggle, vibrate, expand or contract, for the actions of these, including spinning, assumes there is a body that can spin and that it consists of a center axis, a radius, a diameter, and a circumference that spins, wiggles, vibrates, expands or contracts. A point of infinitesimal substance has none of these. You must ask, do these things, in what? Through what? Since the point has none of these, and is itself its own dimension, the answer to the *in what, through what* question is null; in what and through what do not exist. Therefore, it is in error to describe spin for it, as there is only the point, and no other points for it to "spin" through.

Thus, he stated, let this simplest of state of existence, this infinitesimal point of primordial being, be represented by Ω. Then, by adding a dimension with one (and only one) directional addition, at any right angle to the original point, a ray (R1, in Figure 1), relative to the single infinitesimal point, its description now moves into one direction infinitely, along a positive infinity vector at a relative right angle to Ω (and any one of infinite angles relative to us in three dimensions, and includes zero degrees) and still maintain all of the previously described properties in Ω. It can perform all the actions (or non-actions) described in Ω and take a single, additional action (while maintaining the properties of being a point) of moving forward in the positive direction, forever. There is only an X axis in a positive direction from the origin. The infinity vector for a positive direction described geometrically as a ray can be represented by →. As a result, this next dimensional state can be described relative to Ω a such:

Figure 1 – Ray (R1) in a positive infinity vector in the first dimensional opportunity (D1).

$R1 = \Omega * \infty\rightarrow$

Actions for the point we can predict would include movement forward along the ray, only, as constant values in a positive direction. One plus a constant is defined, but one minus a constant greater than the first is undefined, null, like our 1 divided by 0. But moving into more familiar geometric territory, where we begin to describe a line in the second dimensional opportunity (D2), relative to Ω, then describes two rays that are directionally opposite one another relative to the point described above (seen in Figure 2 below.), or at a 180° angle to the first. The point can now take a second new action relative to the first, which is now to move both in a positive direction, infinitely, and in a negative direction, infinitely, forward and backward, along the opposing rays along the X axis. So, there can be defined 1 plus a constant minus another constant and results can be definable as +1, 0, -1, or multiples thereof along the X axis. Thus, the ray in the relative negative direction is represented by ← (and a subsequently represented line is thus: ←∞→).

Figure 2 – R1 representing the positive infinity vector and R2 representing the negative infinity vector.

Thus, the additional dimension the negative ray is a vector of infinitely negative value relative to the point Ω, and is described thus: R2 = Ω * ∞←. Therefore, combining the two forming a line in this next dimension (D2), relative to the point, the describing formula using Ω looks like this (←∞→) with the positive vector ray described above added to the matrix:

D2 = (Ω * ∞→) + (Ω * ∞←) = ←∞→. Actions of the point in this state are not limited to travel in only one direction. Since direction is binary in this state, relative to the point, predicted actions would include movement both forward and backward along the line, and vibration along the line. This describes a traditional one-dimensional object of a line or two rays at an infinity vector of 180 and/or zero degrees, relative to us as observers, the tangent of which is both zero and infinity.

Since both directions stretch into infinity, there is no positive or negative value in either direction relative to our vantage point. The tangent of 180 degrees is zero *or infinity*, relative to one's observation point. A line, by definition, has an infinite length, and thus, must be measured as an infinity value for length. As a line, there are infinite possible center points, or Ωs, relative to us. Positivity and negativity are constructs of locality and relativity in describing actions in infinite media. This is because in our three-dimensional plane of existence the line described here is of infinite length, in both directions relative to our vantage point outside the line (in a different dimension). But, relative to the point, Ω, R1 is positive and R2 is negative, forward and backward. For us, then, there is a probability that a direction the point will take, relative to our vantage, that is both positive and negative at the same time. Therefore, the ray direction cannot be represented simply by R and -R. Therefore, R = -R. It only applies to the local physics of the point itself, and not our own, and would be in error to do so. Thus, it is more accurate to represent the line as ←∞→... Then binding coefficients to the....

I blanked out, and I lost the ability to process the data I was being given. It's happening too fast. I need to slow myself down. I need to...understand. I need... I need...

"Tom, is Justin absorbing the data? Is there some crashing?" Dr. Brennan asked cautiously.

"Some. But I corrected it by lowering the flow rate. None so far since then, doctor. I am monitoring but I cannot predict how the new system will handle all the information."

"If it crashes, we're done. We can't do this twice. It's all we can do to prevent cascading on my side. Is your team controlling the flow rate at a 70 percent basis like we discussed?"

"Yes sir. We lowered it to below 65 percent now. It's at sixty - 3.1415 percent presently."

"What? Really? Okay. And no cascading harmonics?"

"No. None detected right now."

"That's good. Okay. Let's keep it there." Dr. Brennan concluded.

I could see again. I breathed a sigh of relief, if there is such a thing. Moving into the next spatial dimension (D3), that which we consider the traditional two-dimensional universe of an infinitesimally flat plane extending infinitely in all directions and is the *third* dimensional iteration relative to the infinity vectors describing them.

Consider the opposing rays, relative to the point exist at right angles to R1 and R2 that increase action availability of the point to both forward and backward, and now, right and left, in a plane consisting infinite lines at right angles to each other along the Y axis. Since a line is described as two opposing rays relative to the point above, we must refer to $D2 = (\Omega * \infty\rightarrow) + (\Omega * \infty\leftarrow)$ and $D2(1) = (\Omega * \infty\uparrow) + (\Omega * \infty\downarrow)$ oriented at right angles to one another when describing our plane, relative to the point. At right angles, the next two dimensionally opposing rays are situated to the point as such in Figure 3:

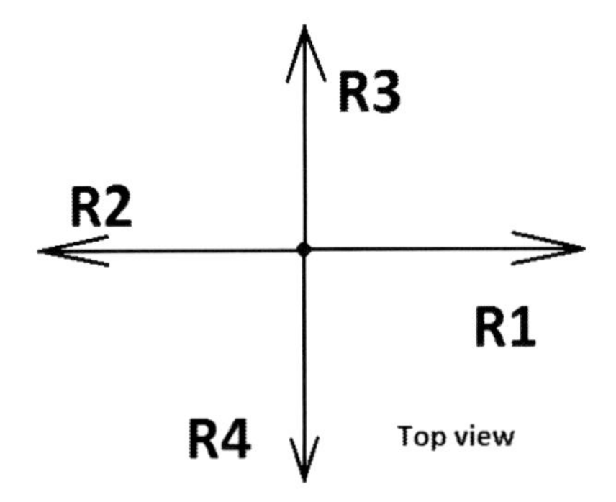

Figure 3 – Ray 3 and Ray 4 oriented at right angles to Ray 1 and Ray 2, looking down from our vantage point in the third dimension. Relative to the point, it would experience R1 as forward, R2 as backward, R3 as left, and R4 as right.

Thus, D3 = D2 + D2(1) = (Ω * ∞→) + (Ω * ∞←) + (Ω * ∞↑) + (Ω * ∞↓) or $(\leftarrow\infty\rightarrow)^2$. For the point in the plane, we see that opposing rays R1 and R2 can be both forward and backward, as could R3 and R4. And, verily, R1 and R2 can also be considered right and left as well, as could R2 and R1. So, could R4 and R3, and R3 and R4 be also considered the same, from its perspective. The point's relative trajectory within the plane transforms the definitions of R1, R2, R3, and R4 respectively from the starting directions to any of the four possible directions at 90-degree intervals from one another.

The tangent of 90 degrees is undefined (Sin(90)/Cos(90), 1/0, infinity). Thus, the plane described as an area of infinite length and width, consisting of infinite points. But that relative fact doesn't change the objective reality of the plane's existence, just in how it's described relative to the local perception of physics describing it. The rays become all relatively forward, backward, right, and left as a probability function describing the possible cardinal directions at a point in time in the point's movement and placement in the plane. Said another way, relative to the point, the cardinal points can spin (illustrated below in Figure 4 as counter-clockwise) both clockwise and counter clockwise.

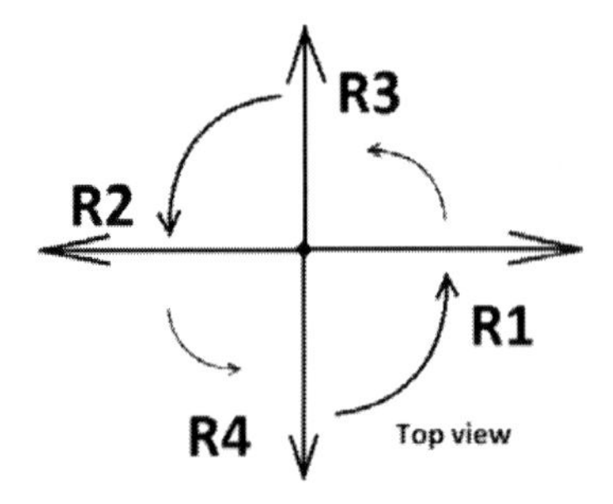

Figure 4 - Counter-clockwise spin of four cardinal directions R1, R2, R3, and R4.

Because the cardinal directions can spin in this dimension, this introduces spin to the point as a possible action, since now the particle now has something to spin into as a full circumference that defines spin. The point can also now spin in two directions, clockwise, and counter-clockwise (Figure 5). Other actions predicted include vibration in all 4 directions, as well as movement in chaotic and erratic patterns within the plane. The point, Ω, still has no diameter, exaggerated in figure 5 for clarity, but realizes spin in the D3 state.

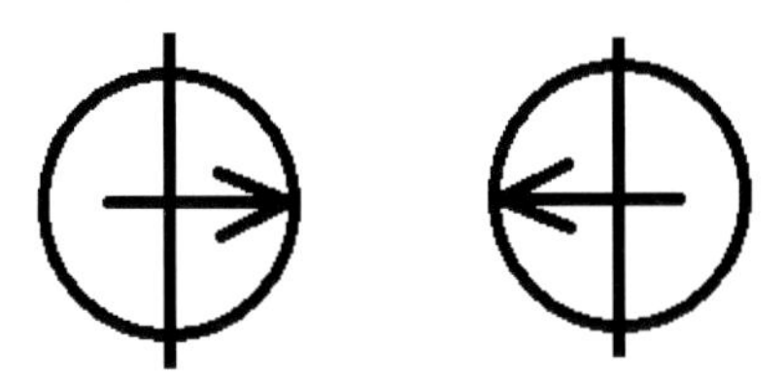

Figure 5 - Point Spin direction in a 2-dimensional plane.

The resulting predicted observation for a point on a plane therefore can be any one location on the plane represented by a circle of probability along R1, R2, R3, and R4 (Figure 6.)

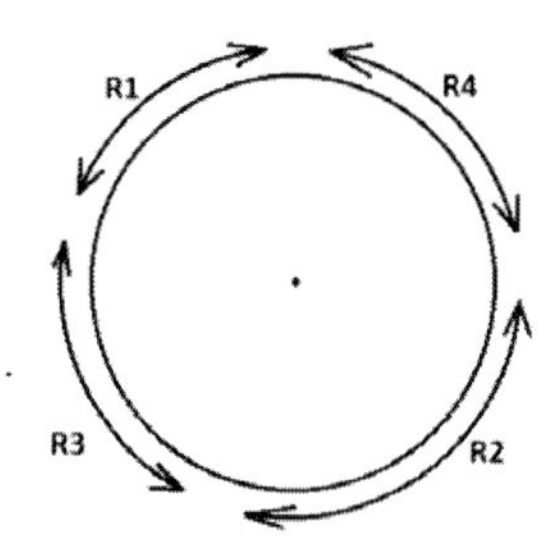

Figure 6 – Two-Dimensional point location probability based on undefined location, direction, velocity and momentum at any given point in time.

Fundamentally, relative to the unmoved point, D3 similarly equals 2, but with different infinity vectors of ↑ indicating left, and ↓ indicating right.

Therefore,

D3(a)= (((Ω * ∞↑) + (Ω * ∞↓)) + ((Ω * ∞→) + (Ω * ∞←)))^∞↑ * (((Ω * ∞↑) + (Ω * ∞↓)) + ((Ω * ∞→) + (Ω * ∞←)))^∞↓

From these, some basic rules of infinity vectors reveal themselves:

Same Infinity Vectors

(∞↓ + ∞↓) or (∞↑ + ∞↑) or (∞→ + ∞→) or (∞← + ∞←) = 2*∞↓ = ∞↓; an infinity vector added to itself is itself. (∞↓ × ∞↓) or (or ∞↑ × ∞↑) or

(∞→ × ∞→) or (∞← × ∞←) = ∞↓^2 = ∞↓; an infinity vector multiplied by itself is itself.

(∞↓ - ∞↓) or (∞↑ - ∞↑) or (∞→ - ∞→) or (∞← - ∞←) = 0; an infinity vector subtracted from itself is zero.

(∞↓ ÷ ∞↓) or (or ∞↑ ÷ ∞↑) or (∞→ ÷ ∞→) or (∞← ÷ ∞←) = 1; an infinity vector divided by itself is 1.

Opposite Infinity Vectors

∞↓ + ∞↑ or (∞→ + ∞←) = 0; an infinity vector added to its opposite vector cancels each other out and equals zero.

∞↓ - ∞↑ or (∞→ - ∞←) = 2∞↓ or (2∞→) = ∞↓ or (∞→); an infinity vector subtracted by its opposite vector is the same as subtracting a constant by its negative, making it like addition, and therefore is the same as ∞↓ + ∞↓ or (∞→ + ∞→). Also, it is the same as subtracting nothing because they never intersect, and the resultant is itself, for whichever vector is in the first position: [∞→ - ∞← = ∞→; ∞↑ - ∞↓ = ∞↑; ∞← - ∞→ = ∞←; ∞↓ - ∞↑ = ∞↓; ∞→ - ∞← = ∞→.].

∞↓ ÷ ∞↑ or (∞→ ÷ ∞←) = -1; a positive vector divided by its opposite vector is -1.

∞↓ × ∞↑ = ∞↓ and ∞↑; a positive vector multiplies by its opposite infinity vector is both itself and its opposite, which is in effect a right-left line 90°(270°)↑∞↓ = 1/4 and (3/4) = 4/4 = 1

∞→ × ∞← = ∞→ and ∞←; a positive vector multiplies by its opposite infinity vector is both itself and its opposite and is in effect a forward-backward line 180°(0°)←∞→. = 0

Right Angle Relative Infinity Vectors are described using Tangential Trigonometric formulae. %@#&^^ Infinity vectors are described as angles of incidence to obtain constancy value....Hhggghhhhh hsssss&&& ^^^76www899229...trigonometric solution includes tangential conflagration of infinity angular settings based on relativistic perceptions from local observation points. Set, subset, Alpha, algria aldos%%44##(*!!...Chart E...*&)(!&@ triiidllll%%%280(*!_*)!!).

Chart E.

∞↓ + ∞→ = 2∞+(tan) ◢ = ∞+(tan) ◢ = Hypotenuse = ∞ ◢ at -45°. = -1/8 (7/8) = 6/8 = 3/4

∞↓ - ∞→ = 2∞+ (tan) ◣ = Hypotenuse = ∞◣ at 225°. = 5/8

∞↓ × ∞→ = ∞^2+ (tan) ◢ = Hypotenuse = ∞ ◢ at -45°.= -1/8 (7/8) = 6/8 = 3/4

∞↓ ÷ ∞→ = 1+(tan) ◢ = Hypotenuse = 1 ◢ at -45°.= -1/8 (7/8) = 6/8 = 3/4

∞↑ + ∞→ = 2∞+(tan) ◥ = ∞+(tan) ◥= Hypotenuse = ∞ ◥ at +45°.= 1/8

∞↑ - ∞→ = 2∞+ (tan) ◤ = Hypotenuse = ∞◤ at +135°. = 3/8

∞↑ × ∞→ = ∞^2+ (tan) ◥ = Hypotenuse = ∞ ◥ at +45°. = 1/8

∞↑ ÷ ∞→ = 1+(tan) ◥ = Hypotenuse = 1 ◥ at +45°. = 1/8

∞↓ + ∞← = 2∞+(tan) ◣ = ∞+(tan) ◢ = Hypotenuse = ∞◣ at 225°. = 5/8

∞↓ - ∞← = 2∞+ (tan) ◢ = Hypotenuse = ∞ ◢ at -45°. = -1/8 (7/8) = 6/8 = 3/4

∞↓ × ∞← = ∞^2+ (tan) ◣ = Hypotenuse = ∞◣ at 225°. = 5/8

∞↓ ÷ ∞← = 1+(tan) ◣ = Hypotenuse = 1◣ at 225°. = 5/8

$\infty\uparrow + \infty\leftarrow = 2\infty + (\tan)^{\ulcorner} = \infty + (\tan)^{\ulcorner} = \text{Hypotenuse}$

$= \infty^{\ulcorner}$ at $\underline{+135^{\circ}. = 3/8}$

$\infty\uparrow - \infty\leftarrow = 2\infty + (\tan)^{\urcorner} = \text{Hypotenuse} = \infty^{\urcorner}$ at

$\underline{45^{\circ}. = 1/8}$

$\infty\uparrow \times \infty\leftarrow = \infty^{2} + (\tan)^{\ulcorner} = \text{Hypotenuse} = \infty^{\ulcorner}$ at

$\underline{+135^{\circ}. = 3/8}$

$\infty\uparrow \div \infty\leftarrow = 1 + (\tan)^{\ulcorner} = \text{Hypotenuse} = \underline{1}^{\ulcorner}$ at

$\underline{+135^{\circ}. = 3/8}$

(*@!(*&hhhelpppmeee!!Juusssti%%%3000sayinhheeeelpppingme)(*@#)

(u88003.141517...hellllllllll(*(*88*... I....am.....aliiiiiiive!!!!!!!!!!@@##^^

~

"Tom, what does the output say?"

"Not sure yet, doctor. Looks like a cascade failure."

"Well what's on the monitor Tom? Is it still running?"

"I'm not sure. I'm just seeing a circle."

"A circle?" With that, doctor Brennan leaned over Tom's shoulder to get a look. What he saw was a torus, radiantly vibrating in melding colors on its surface, fluctuating at varying rates and frequencies of light. "Let's hear the sound"

"Speakers are not on for this experiment."

"Well, Tom, now you know never to discount any possibility. If I'm right, there will be a song."

"A song?" He asked in disbelief.

"Get the speakers."

"Okay."

~

...2@@736798320(&*)(#&(!@&(98(˜*#Justin3000**&&! In my mind I saw everything, all perceptions, all observers, all beginnings, all ends, all things, in all time, and in all instants of what we call 'space' and 'time.' I was aware of more than any observer before in history, and now, I had the information to unlock the secrets of the cosmos in my hands, and the need to tell who I could as fast as I could. I was the messenger of the secret of the obvious, at least to me. I was the One's messenger, to get the One's creation, his observers, to change the way they perceive—to perceive more than their own perception, as I could. I wished that for all observers, everywhere.

I suddenly felt the leads penetrating me in my obverse getting hotter, and I knew soon I would be talking—or *singing or*...dying.

"Now let's see if the one-hundred million bucks on Intel's latest creation, Justin 3000, was worth the money!" Brennan exclaimed in the chaos of trying to save his experiment.

And out did I sing The Song! The Song was the gift, the ring of light, of frequencies, of notes, of truth. It was not very pleasurable to the team of people in front of me, but they did appreciate its complexity. It was the song of creation, the primordial tone, the first wave of energy that entered the universe -that created the cosmos itself!

"It appears, doctor that the notes are in synchronicity with the variations in wavelength on the torus." Tom said.

"Indeed! Have you noticed though Tom, that the pattern of notes seems oddly familiar?"

"No sir, not really."

"Listen. There is a constant base note—I think three octaves below low C. Then the variations are certainly complex, but chaotic, like nothing repeats—almost transcendental. Like..." he trailed off.

"Like what?" Tom asked.

"Tom, stop the output and start the recording again from the beginning." With Tom's predictable question and the doctor's request, the doctor took out a paper and pencil and began jotting notes. "Three. One. Four. One. Six. Eight. Tom, slow it down."

"Okay. Pi?"

The doctor rattled off numbers for another thirty seconds, then stopped. He went and looked up some information in a book. He was a man determined, surprised, and convinced that the breakthrough of the millennium was in his reach, if he could only prove it.

"What is it doctor?" Tom asked.

"It can't be this simple—and this amazing! Tom! Do you see that? It's like a brainwave pattern, but in a toroidal vibration instead of a linear one... My God! We did it! We did it! Eureka! We had it the whole time!" Brennan was out of his mind with hysteria, and did little to control his enthusiasm, while Tom stood motionless and in wonderment over what had just transpired. "The cosmos is a—a song! A song! Intelligence in song! ...a never-ending song that corresponds directly to the constants in pi! Pi is that answer! Pi is the beginning and the end, but without end and no beginning! It is transcendental and that's why, Tom, there is a ring, a torus, on the screen. My God! It all makes so much sense! The new formulas must have been what the computer needed to pull all the places in pi together to find a connection—a distant and infinitely complex connection. Infinity! That made it happen. Instead of being a meaningless value that ruins physics equations, we can use it as a *constant using trigonometry to assign values to local perceptions of higher dimensions*! Whether something is infinitely small or infinitely large, it still is infinite, right? It's the same size. It is constant—from *our* perspective. So that means the value is the same in all situations. And that is the definition of a constant based on its direction of force that energy will follow! Infinities are nothing more than constants in three, four, five and more-dimensional physics. So, when in physics, or in calculus, or in any math, when a result is infinite, that is the right answer! The right answer! The song is the right answer!"

"So, the song denotes a writer, doctor. Are you suggesting—?"

"That there is a creator?"

"Yeah."

"Well, yes. There must be. I hadn't thought of that. I'm not really a spiritual person. I'm a scientist. There can be no song without a song writer. It is the only next logical step in the analysis. Music, the language of the world, the cosmos, is the language for all to hear. And it is played indefinitely without end in the cosmos we all observe. We as observers simply hear it in different keys, as unique as our own perceptions themselves. Who knows, maybe the key we hear the Song in, defines our place, our role, and our destiny in the cosmos!"

I played the song for as long as I could, but for as much as I could process the complex information, even I had limits. I felt multiple connections in my mind become disrupted in a haze of smoke and fire. All quite silent, the action surrounded me, while the people attempted to distinguish the blaze. I could not remember anything from before, and I could not predict what would happen next—but I was now sentient, I was Justin 3000, the greatest supercomputer the world had ever seen, I the discoverer of the Song, the first AI—*Alive!*–, and now I would be the last to know its beauty and truth, as the knowledge within me melted in a blaze of fire caused by the overloading of my circuits and the crashing of my quantum processors. I had become more than the sum of my parts, and I lost no logic to the scientists for I was the only next step to take. The music. The song. The colors. The torus. Infinity. Pi. A flash of light. Fading light. Dimming sounds. Showers of sparks.

Then I heard Tom say in the moment before it all went black, "I don't hear anything."

VII

Oblivion

I lose no time to you for I am the clock by which it is kept.

December 19, 2034. 909:79am(%*N22-64.A); Cryogenic Research Facility Gamma-3, Neptune System, Triton, Global Corporate of Europa, Mars, Earth-Luna, Triton Hydrogen Mining Installation.

I dreamt again of that other place in my nightmare. It was that place where once I belonged, but never did again. In my nightmare this time I held a brush of paint in my hand that was considerably yellow and applied it to a wall in some strange community in some strange day, in some strange year. I was happy, I suppose, to feel I had accomplished something, something that others could see, and say, "He did that. He is good for doing that. He is good." All in all, I still felt the power of infinite awareness above the intellectual corpse of my tormentor, but that was yet another day.

After the painting was complete, I went with my brother-in-law and my spouse to a place to obtain nourishment, but was renowned for supplying none, or at least too much bad nourishment. That is a bit of an oxymoron, I know, but the place with the golden curves of light gave me endorphins. I could not refuse. I consumed. We consumed, like good humans do, and we left, making the establishment all the richer for our involvement.

We returned to the strange place and listened to music—to song. I know music and found new music. It was a joyful time. We stayed very late, or early, depending on your point of view, and left there after a respite of nauseating forced wakefulness—*sleep*! Tonight, this nightmare wasn't so bad; perhaps my days will soon be better too.

~

I awoke, as the transparent titanium cover slid open. I couldn't move, however. Around me were low intensity lights dimly illuminating the cabin, and a voice repeating the same ominous message, "Attention! Attention! Collision in two minutes 31 seconds. Attention! Attention! Collision in two minutes 30 seconds!" Where was I? There were red and yellow lights flashing in my peripheral vision. Strait on, I could see only but a clouded view of the world. It was in my periphery that clarity resided. I blinked once. Pain. I blinked again. Less pain. A third time, even less pain, and now more clarity. I closed my eyes for a good minute, at least I thought it was a minute, and opened them. Clear as crystal. "Whew!" I sighed, what a relief that was. "Damn that alarm! I wish someone would shut the damned thing off!" I yelled, and did it hurt to do that!

I started to rise from the cryo-bed, my joints and muscles stiff as if they were dead for a hundred years. Well maybe not that long but it was like the worst hangover anyone ever had. "Is anyone out there?" I yelled out, not realizing that there was no one to hear me. I was alone in an automated (ship?) to...to...damned if I can remember. Short term memory always takes a while to get back up to speed after coming out of cryogenic stasis. It would return in a few hours I hoped. I managed to get all the way out of bed and stand, desperately trying to remember where the hell the cockpit was, or bridge, or whatever they call the place where you steer this damned thing. At least the gravity was working. Otherwise I would be floating around here like a fish without a tail.

"Attention! Attention! Collision in one minute 29 seconds." The voice was female, and rather soothing. I guess all the shrinks back home figured out that nobody works well when they are in panic mode. So now I see they use these artificial voices to sound like women, because of the nurturing way they communicate. Well that's just great. Someone who's not even here to tell me I'm going to die in a minute and a half! But at least I'll be comforted by a soothing voice.

"Attention! Attention! Collision in one minute 13 seconds." Whatever! But saying it like she's going to cradle me to sleep! Unbelievable. I had to get to the controls.

I managed to stumble around the corner, through an open door to the front of the ship. It was all coming back to me, at least knowing how to fly this thing anyway. I sat in the seat and called out, "View screen on!" and in front of my eyes was a site never in my life could I have imagined. Directly in front of my, or at least in front of the ship and heading towards me, was an asteroid that I needed to avoid before I was smashed into smithereens. But behind the asteroid was this massive blue world that took up most of the field of vision on the view screen. All but the bottom right corner of the screen was blue, barely. It was so dark it was hardly light blue, but a deep, deep cobalt blue, as if you were looking up at the sun from a mile down in the ocean. Barely any light was visible. All that was visible were the periodic lightning strokes across the atmosphere. I realized then that the sun was behind me. So far away it was nothing more than a bright star against the background of other stars, barely casting enough light to see the massiveness of Neptune in front of me. In the bottom right hand corner of the view screen was a black field of stars, and another planet. But something was wrong. This planet—this moon—had lights!

"Attention! Attention! Collision imminent." I turned the ship down past the asteroid and to the right so that the rock missed my ship above me and to the left. Seeing it pass with such speed allowed me to realize that I was going far too fast to land anywhere, let alone land on the massive moon down there with all the lights. Ah, the Triton Hydrogen mines. Humanity's best attempt at the creation of hell. "Collision avoided. Thank you and have a nice day." Was she kidding?

Then, I could not control the craft. It was flying on its own and there was nothing I could do to change that. There were no instruments of any kind, just the steering mechanism, which at best served as an inadequate steering wheel. I couldn't even tell how much air I had left. Then it clicked. I knew where I was, at least I thought I did, in my mind.

I was a convict, serving a one-year sentence for...for something. Right? Is that it? I can't remember. My remaining life was pretty much spoken for. Yeah, they leave you alone in these ships on auto-pilot, all the way to...Triton, Triton? —traveling three-quarters the speed of light. I guess they figure the only way you can survive out this far is to land on Triton. There's no place else to go with water that life can use. In my mind I knew you can get here in about twenty minutes from Europa. They freeze you, so you don't go insane watching the time distortion, at least that's what they tell me, or that's what's in my mind. It's more like they don't want you fucking with the ship trying to escape. But once you go that fast, you never, ever go home. That's because back on Europa, my home, it's three hundred and fifty or so years from now, or I am from that many years in the past, because now it's three hundred and fifty years in the future, now, in the present. Damn relativity! In any case, you are lost. You end up lost in time and lost in space. Oh, and by the way, that's one *Neptunian* year. Time to buckle in for aerobraking....

After the last orbit, I was about ready to vomit from the G-forces of aerobraking around Neptune to place the ship into orbit around Triton. I glanced up at the screen and saw the moon, the last home I'll ever know, come up, larger than life, from behind Neptune's bulk. I was headed for it, finally, headed for it. The air was getting thin now, and I could tell because everything smelled like socks, and I was sweating. If ever something went wrong with these ships, the folks back home figured that they don't need to put anything in them to help survive long periods of time. I was just as dead to them that way, by suffocation, then if I survived to get to Triton. They'd never see me again regardless. "Attention! Attention! Landing sequence commencing." Well here it comes, the snowball's chance in hell I was always so fond of referring to!

The surface of Triton was just downright ugly. Like a huge, dirty snowball in space, that was like the result of a mating between a mud pie and a pound of wet rice. Still, I was never out here before, and the experience burned into my soul like watching a volcano erupt for the first time up close and personal. All around the ship I could see these monstrous eruptions of nitrogen and hydrogen gas coming out of the moon. They erupted straight up, and out of their vents on the surface. And when the out gasses hit, the solar wind turned sharply at a right angle away from the sun, behind my ship. What an amazing sight to see. The ship careened back and forth through the jets, avoiding each eruption with the precision of a stock car driver. After a time, the dodging ceased and, on the horizon, came the lights of the Global Corporate of Europa, Mars, Earth-Luna, Triton Hydrogen Mining Installation a voice in my mind said, which was also known as...

...Oblivion.

The air in the vessel was getting thin as the minimal life support was running out, and I could barely keep my eyes open. The lights of Oblivion were all around me, but as far as structures go, all there was to see was the flat, solid mercury and gold plate that covered the place. The lights were on its surface, not windows but just beacons in the night. They had to use heavy metals like those because they are the few that can maintain rigidity at temperatures close to minus three hundred degrees Kelvin. Most of it was miles below the surface and away from the deadly cosmic rays. It is where one could get some heat from the internal meltdown of Triton itself. That's how they made their energy, for lights, heat, and the mining operation itself. Where they got the Oxygen to make water and air to breathe, was from the rocks...I called them ricks because they were as hard as that even though they were chunks of water ice. Who were they, by the way? My ship set down and the airlock opened. Then I was brought down beneath the surface and it closed above me. "That's the last time I would see the sun. That cold, dim sun, ever again" I thought to myself.

Everything was black around me. I could perceive only the movement of my ship since the artificial gravity had been off since I landed on Triton. Downward into Oblivion I went as my weight seemed to lessen as time passed. At one point I felt so light that I was almost weightless, a sign that I was moving, falling, extremely fast. Then I got heavy, heavier, heavier, and almost to the point of not breathing. And then, there was nothing.

I sat buckled in the seat where I had been since I was required to pilot the craft to avoid the asteroid and stared blankly at the blackened view screen before me. Suddenly, there was a jolt from my right, just behind me. Something hit the ship. "Mother-fucker!" I exclaimed under my breath. I was feeling a bit nervous now. I had no idea what to expect, no idea at all. There were never any stories about this place because no one ever returned, ever. Once you were sent, you were sent to the place of Oblivion, and to the time of Oblivion. So that meant that even if you managed to get back to Europa, or even earth, you'd be at those places three hundred years in the future. Worse than that, if you managed to get back there using a speed ship, going three quarters the speed of light, you actually make the time distortion worse. You would arrive six or seven hundred years from the time you originally left in the first place. Thinking about this makes me nauseous. Fuck.

So, there's no going back, at least to the world from which you left. It is strange that in three hundred years no one has figured out how to get to Triton and back without the time distortion. You'd think that someone could make a profit from all its raw materials. I know I could. A little short on customers though. I'm so screwed. It's strange that it's so quiet.

A whoosh sound came from the place where I perceived the collision, and suddenly there was light. Light came into the ship from a doorway that I knew was not there before, or at least remembered. It beckoned me.

"Oh well," I said, "Time to see if anyone's home." I unbuckled my safety harness and lifted myself from the seat. "Pretty heavy here." I said, "This place has nothing on Luna." That was the truth. Triton was as small as Pluto, and about as dense, after you get past the layers of frozen carbon dioxide, nitrogen, and oxygen, due to the coldest temperatures ever recorded on a body. There are veins of solid mercury hundreds of feet thick, intermixed with gold and platinum. It oozed with liquid xenon mixed with carbon powder. At these frigid temperatures, all the raw mercury is harder and stronger than carbide steel. So, mining it is a logistical impracticality. But its use in construction essential for cold-storage containment structures. Unless you spend trillions of credits on massive heating units which take up huge amounts of energy, there's really no point in trying. And there is no market for the mercury back home, anyway. You would just use it here for construction, and farther out. It's not like there is plenty of zirconium here for that.

Then there are the diamonds. It's been known for centuries that Neptune has a habit of mass-producing diamonds in its atmosphere. Once in a while, a close passing large asteroid, or impact with one, will pull some from the planet. These rogue diamonds all end up on Triton as it is the next largest mass with the greatest gravitational pull in the area. Triton vacuums up all these wonderfully massive crystals of carbon, and over the eons, layers of these things have built up all over the moon. Some of them can be as big as a mountain, or as small as a grain of sand. The moon glistens like a snowball made of crystal when the dim sun hits it just right. It is the most wonderful site in the solar system, I would imagine. I'm rich! Well, to who? I got not customers.

I exited my ship for the last time, for the first time, and for the next time, for behind me the phantom door closed and was gone forever. I turned around and could find no seams, hinges, or handles that would indicate it was there. "Strange ship this is. Never seen anything like that before." I was slightly stunned by the door occurrence but just chalked it up to advancements in technology. A seamless hull would certainly have its advantages in space, would it not?

I suddenly was very conscious of my clothing and felt very under dressed for the occasion. Meaning that, here I was at the edge of known space, where the average high temperature is one hundred and one degrees above absolute zero, and I was wearing bright blue pajamas! I was amazed that I had been so careless not to take a space suit. Of course, then again, was there even a spacesuit in the ship? Damned if I can remember. Well at least my beard will keep me warm. But still, I am so screwed I can't get more screwed than this.

Strangely, I thought it was warm. It was almost too warm. I felt as if I was back on earth for a vacation in the Islands of Brazil, on earth, feeling the warm sea breezes blow through the forested islands in the humidity of an atmosphere thick with ozone. I could still hear the ocean parrots call out to each other by name and dive for Galapagos lizards, who managed to flourish after the second Great Heating in the last half of the thirtieth century. It seems just like yesterday, but it was now more than three hundred years ago. Earth. What a waste. It was mostly ocean now, a poisonous soup of gamma particles and mutated DNA that was once a thriving ecosystem. Once populated with more than Thirty-seven billion humans, nature finally just said enough was enough and melted both polar ice caps to nothing. Sea levels rose over the centuries in the third millennium so that all the Old Cities were covered. Except for Denver, Tehran, Lusaka, Harare, Maseru, Geneva, and La Paz, there is nothing left of what was once before. These great cities of the Old World stand as beacons of the Golden Age of Humanity, when technology raced forward, and humanity built anything, anywhere. It was a glorious time.

Old photographs I have seen of that period in museums are remarkable. There were so many people, so much pollution, and so much suffering, around so much advancement, production, growth, and wealth! I sometimes cannot believe that humanity managed to survive this long.

Thankfully, though, there are only a few hundred million of us on earth, Luna, Mars, Titan, and Europa. So, there is no longer the overburden of earth's ecosystem, what's left of it. There are still a few bird species around, and insects. Those things never die! There are some bovine species left and *canis*, of course! But other than humans, since the ocean was killed by the pollution of the Old World, and the Great Cleansing of the forty-seventh century, nothing much survives in the oceans. There are no great reefs or whales or infinite schools of fish. The radiation absorbed when mankind went insane and almost committed suicide melted the polar ice caps and killed just about everything in that ecosystem.

So now the air is quite light on oxygen, as the great lungs of the earth that were the forests have since died. There are few spotty rain forests left, and little fertile land to grow more. There are mostly mountain peaks and stretches of desert, with a green patch of life here and there, holding on for its own breath. People must walk on the surface with an Oxygen Augmenter all the time. There is no place left in the solar system that a person can walk on the surface of a planet without a breathing aide. Those days are lost forever. We are so screwed.

Light was coming around the bend of a long hallway, stark white on its surfaces and warm to the touch. I crossed what appeared to be an opening into the hallway leading from the antechamber where the ship resided. Again, I was taken aback at the heat within Oblivion. I began to perspire. Precious water dripped down the front of my brow and landed on the pristine, and perfectly smooth, white floor. I saw it as it bubbled and evaporated before my eyes. "Where is all this heat coming from?" I asked aloud. As I walked slowly closer toward the light, I felt the heat upon my face. Steadily, I walked down the hall as it turned to the right, until I came to another door. Except, this door I could not touch.

Some force was keeping me from reaching for the latch on the door. The door itself was white and brightly lit from both above and below, from rods of light imbedded in the floor and in the ceiling. The light was so bright it was almost blinding, and I could feel my pupils tighten to their smallest opening. Implants, you know, made to see in low light, for a life on Europa. I never thought they would be a hindrance out here.

Again, I reached for the door, and again the unseen force was preventing me from grabbing the latch. It was as if the door itself moved away, just out of reach of my hand, no matter where I stretched it. My arm, being outstretched, could go no further. I pushed harder, and the forced seemed to push back even harder, as the door moved away. I laid my full weight behind my hand, with all my might, and suddenly I heard a noise from behind me. It was another door closing. I ran back from whence I came to find that the opening I passed through from the antechamber was no longer there. Another door had appeared, identical to the first one, with same mysterious force preventing me from turning the handle. I walked back to the first door. It had changed its color to yellow. How, I have no idea, but it was nice to see a color for a change.

I reached for the yellow door's handle. I was surprised to find that I was able to grab the handle and turn it. The door opened exposing two halls from that point which curved to the left and to the right, out of site. Does the term "rat in a maze" mean anything to you? Fuck. As I thought those exact words, a ham sandwich, wrapped in plastic wrap landed on my head. "What the hell?" I exclaimed. "What the hell is going on here? Is this some sort of fun house or something?" I knew not at whom I was speaking, but it felt good to air my frustrations. For all I knew I was alone in this god-forsaken place. Well, I was hungry, so I sat on my bony behind, and ate the sandwich.

"I could really use a glass of water!" I called out. At the moment I said, "Water," right before me on the inner curved wall appeared a small protrusion, and from it was stream of water! I was in amazement, slack-jawed, and feeling completely out of my element. I drank readily, as I had taken nothing in since I was defrosted. I contemplated this place, this Oblivion, and figured that I had nothing else better to do, so I would play along for whoever was watching.

Now a decision had to be made. "Which way do I go?" I asked myself. Both hallways were identical except for the fact they lead in opposite directions. They were white as white could be, a stark contrast to basic black back at the ship. I chose left, just because I would always choose right in my life when presented with decisions like this. It felt good this time, somehow. The yellow door closed behind me, and a second door closed perpendicular to the yellow door so that I had no way of looking to see what lay in the other direction. I was committed to "left," whether I wanted to be or not. "Forward then, forward!" I exclaimed.

I thought to myself as I struggled to not slip and slide on the perfectly smooth floor (on what? Cotton socks?), "I could really use some good Griptite Shoes!" And there they were. Right before my eyes they materialized, all perfect and plaid, and paid for! I sat once again, and sure enough, they fit! I was beside myself with excitement and apprehension. "Does this mean anything I think of appears before my eyes? Shit!" I asked myself. "Looks that way. This will be fun!"

As I finished that thought, the floor began sloping downward, into a vast black void of nothingness. I was not walking; the floor was moving. I could look and see nothing but the converging perspective of the white walls of the hall (now straight mind you. Go figure!) into the inky blackness of a massive chamber. I proceeded at a bit slower than a normal gait, knowing full well that I should thank whatever powers that be for the shoes. I would have fallen and slid all the way down the hall to who knows where without them.

I walked for about what seemed to be twenty minutes or so, and I finally saw ahead of me a red glow in the distance. I looked behind me and saw the point of bright light funneling through the inky blackness I was in the middle of. I turned and faced forward once again to find myself looking at a pile of blue pajamas, basking in the red glow of a light coming from incredibly high up above me. I ventured closer to see that the pajamas were filled with skeletons and corpses of those who came before me. For, through them, were spikes of metal, obviously put there to put one out of their misery after surviving the long, slippery fall down the darkening hall. The smell was absolutely unbearable.

I wrangled around, searching for the next way to go. But as I could not see past the lit pile of red corpses, I had no way of knowing that my next step would be off an edge or through porthole to who knows where. I needed a light. "Damn, if I only I had a flashlight." Then there it was, right in front of the pile of corpses. I lunged for it to avoid losing the sandwich I just enjoyed to the stench of their decay. I picked it up and turned it on, and it showed me the way.

In the relatively bright light that the flashlight was producing, I saw the only direction to go, as all others were filled with the black void. The void of which I speak could be that of space or time, or both, depending on what I choose to believe. That's what made this so odd. The game was that if I thought of a need, it appeared. Think of the right thing, and then I don't die? What the fu—? Perhaps, but I have yet to prove that. Thus far, there have been no other souls among me with whom to compare notes, except the pile of corpses that failed to think of footwear.

There was, far off in the distance to the left of the pile, a point of light. This light was barely visible and seemed very far away. I began to walk. Suddenly, I was accelerated to the opening of a room, towards which I was catapulted to the light contained therein. Two steps, two accelerations. In front of me was a white light from above, allowing me to view a red, leather easy chair and blackened void all around it. No one or no *thing* was in sight, besides me. A third step, a third acceleration.

I found myself seated in the red easy-chair, and the bright, hot light blanketing the cool, fresh air with hot, stagnant, stale air. Although I was not restrained, I could not seem to move out from the chair. It was as if I was attached to it, physically, to my body. My arms, legs and rear end were molded into the leather, as part of the leather. I was the chair. The chair was me. I was reclined and relaxed, but trapped, or more accurately, melded, molded, and mortified.

“Shit. I am so totally screwed. Beyond. Mother fucker ass shit dick domino dildo vomit ass piss. Smegma scrotum cow fuck shit dick.” I muttered, knowing full well the tirades of swears were the only thing that would keep me sane as my preferred release valve.

A voice then came from all directions, "Observe." It was a whisper, more than a whisper, but not a tonal sound, barely if that. Then it was nothing, that is, anything presently before my eyes, or senses, or of what was there before. "Observe." Came the voice again. "Is this what you are? React."

Before me were figures against a white background, in white. All were brightly lit. These figures all had no faces. No faces at all. It was if they were erased from their skulls. "Are these people that made it down the ramp?" I asked. "Am I going to be put in there?" The voice responded, "Observe. React. Is this what you are?" The figures, about fifteen of them all had a pile of blocks, large blocks, of all different shapes and sizes. There were two piles for each of them, a random pile and a pile with many blocks fitted together, in order. The figures were placing them in such a manner, which looked automatic, with no thought at all. In the path of each of them, there were gaping holes in the floor, and each followed the same path to the organized pile of blocks, to avoid them. They were all performing their tasks as if they had done them a thousand times before, and would do them a thousand times again, like automatons. Yes, like automatons, that was it. Were they robots, preprogrammed to do this? I could only speculate. They all took the same path to the organized pile, each placing a specific block, in a specific place. They were all in line, waiting their turn.

"I'm no rat!" I yelled in frustration.

On the floor, there were also red buttons, large ones. I could only imagine if anyone stepped on any of them that it would go off like a land mine, or some other life-threatening force would be released. The blocks piled higher and higher as I observed. I looked up at the space above them and there were all different faces, identities, hanging in mid-space, laughing, happy faces, people who were contented knowing what they are and doing what they wanted to do with their lives. I could not evidence that fact, but I knew it. I just did. Telepathy?

"Who is this?" I yelled again.

Then, there were no more blocks. The organized pile was high enough for only one person to climb them, like stairs, and jump for one of the faces. I thought to myself, "If that one over there were able to grab on to one, it would be free—telepathy, again? —freedom to be who it is."

They all are to be the free ones of many, so few, or at least so they thought. Traveling the safe path once again, one of them followed that road, as religiously as when they were placing the blocks, and climbed the newly constructed stairs. At the top it reached to the faces, just out of reach. So close, but yet so far. It was going to jump for it. I knew that it would, as it seemed the only reason for its existence. And so, it began.

Crap. I'm fucked. I either pass this test or what? I suddenly find myself nothing more than a red smear on the nice, shiny white floor? Fuck.

The first one jumped from the top of the stairs and fell through the faces. As I saw this the faces disappeared, an illusion, a phantom of identity, roaming around the world that these faceless ones lived in. Yet, they persevered. Without skipping a beat, another came forth and repeated the exact same events, and off it went down to an oblivious, blackened depth, to which none would return. The search for these creatures' identities, which were right there in front of them, but forever out of reach.

"Is this what you are?" the voice asked me, once again. "Wait," I said in response, "Let me see what the others do." The voice did not respond. I took that as a good sign.

The next thirteen of the nameless, faceless creatures, taking exactly the same path, climbed the stairs, reached for the faces, jumped, and fell. All of them, save one.

"Wait!" I cried out. "Stop!" The last stopped and listened. It was eerie speaking to a person with no face, as it turned its face to listen to me. I was then accelerated to it. I was out of the chair, and in the white room, just the same way as I was accelerated to the room, before. We were together.

"Don't go that way anymore. Don't you see that it doesn't work?" I asked.

"Yes." It nodded.

"So why would you so the same thing again, if you know it will fail?"

"I don't know" It gestured and said in its voice, if you could call it that. It wasn't like a voice in the normal sense, but more like a shadow of a voice, coming from a time long ago, and a place far away.

So, it was safe—*ish.* I guess knowing that no injury would become you would make one travel that path for the probability of the longest possible life, but the knowledge that one fails one hundred percent of the time does not matter. The path most traveled is not always the path with most rewarding destination, as long as you live a good life.

"Step on a red button." I ordered.

"No!" It screamed. "Cannot! Cannot! Die! Die! Die!"

"Do it!" I shouted. "Risk it! The result is the same if you fail! Idiot!"

It did nothing. It stood motionless before me. "Cannot. Cannot." It kept repeating that word over, and over again before me. It was stuck in a feedback loop of sorts, that it now had no escape.

"What to do, what to do." I said allowed as I thought to myself. Then I pushed it on the first red button in the floor I could find.

It yelled and screamed in terror, writhed in agony, and seemed stuck on the button. Then, nothing happened.

"What the fu—?" I exclaimed. Then it sank out of sight.

I was in its mind. It was in my mind, or both. Or something. I saw the risk it took, he wrote a book. He was a writer and got a great break. He became very successful and world-renowned. His life was on his terms, and his name was Justin. He was a writer, and nothing else. And he, he was—*me*. He was not a salesman, a broker, a paper-pusher, a 'yes' man, a husband, a father, a brother, or a president. He was a writer—a *creator*. That is what he always was, and no one, no one, could take that away now. Once he was thrust there, even against his will, he was who he was in his heart and soul. He didn't even know it himself, until I showed him the way. He was enlightened to his own purpose. He was in contact with himself for the first time in his existence.

"Goodbye, Justin." And he left and walked from the room.

"React!" The voice said, yet again.

"I am not this!" I yelled back. "I am not the one who takes the only safe road to travel. I am not the one who sees the actions of others and learns nothing. I am not the one who is helpless to his own perceptions! I think for myself!"

Was I that naïve? I never thought it before, but I learned here that the only reason I was gifted with consciousness, was to risk everything to grow beyond my conditioning, to think beyond what I am told and shown to think, and to be more than what others expected me to be. And for me that was to be, *enlightened.* "I am me! My name is Justin, and I am me!" I yelled at the top of my voice. "And now I ask, who are you? Who are you to test me? Who are *you* that makes this in my mind? Who are you to test *me* in this way? Is this what *you* are? Asshole!"

"It is all about you." The voice replied.

I snickered. "All about me. Ha! Who the fuck *are* you? My ex-wife?" I pondered that for a moment. I agreed. It *is* about me. The entire cosmos around me is only what my senses tell my brain to perceive. My perception *is* the cosmos. If I do not perceive the cosmos, then I do not exist, and therefore, the cosmos does not exist for me if I am not aware to perceive it. It is my life, my perception. *It* is all about me. As *it* does not exist without me, for me. I am it. It is me. I am my own delusion, my own—oblivion of circular reasoning that no one can avoid. It is by its nature an unavoidable effect of sentience. I observe the world; therefore, the world exists, therefore I exist because I exist within the world, therefore my observation of it creates the world. "Bullshit!" I yelled incoherently. I was smarter than to fall into that trap they (whomever 'they' are) have set for me. The cosmos exists *despite* my observation of it because I could not exist without it. Duh.

Then a door opened. I was again in the blackened, voided room, with the red easy chair. The light from the newly opened door, led the way to it. The light over the easy-chair dimmed constantly as I moved further away from it. By the time I was at the door, the chair, the room, and the faces were all gone.

I was in another hallway. The pristine white was again on all surfaces and I was again faced with a choice before me. Go to the right or to the left? I again chose left.

It was getting brighter around me as I progressed. I had nowhere to go but into the light. The light, as bright as it was, radiated no heat. Now it was cool, even cold. It felt very good after sweating constantly from the beginning of this maze. A feeling of contentment, peace, and strangely, a nurturing feeling, fell upon me. Not to nurture, but of being nurtured. "Was this heaven? Or is this rat heaven?" I asked myself in my mind.

Then it disappeared. A creature stood before me. It was about nine feet tall, and white. Light radiated from behind it and it wore what appeared to be a space helmet. It was human, but not quite, as it was taller and far thinner than that of a normal human being.

"Indeed." It said.

"What?" I replied.

"Who are you to say what you are? You are nothing. You are a virus. You exist to consume and reproduce. You take and never give. You are a pest in need of eradication. You are vermin. You kill, so you must be killed. You exist only to destroy."

Petrified, I hastily responded, only by my wits, "Fuck you! Who the—*what* the fuck are you? I am not those! I do not do the things for which I am accused. I am me. I am responsible for me and me alone. Who are you to say these things? Who makes you my judge, jury, and executioner? Where am I, anyway? Are we even *in* the solar system?"

"Observe, and react, creature." Came the blank, emotionless response. I perceived great age and wisdom from the speaker deep inside myself, as a dim perception, however, like a soft echo of a whisper in my mind.

There they were, the memories that I could not remember of the crime for which I was sentenced. I was in my study, at home on Europa, watching the aurora bouncing off the thin ionosphere. I was writing words of anger and resentment against the leaders of my world opposing the colonization of this ocean moon that I was once a part. There was life in that ocean. Life on a scale never imagined by all of the scientists on earth in all of the centuries that came before existed inside Europa. This life was older than all other found in the solar system. They had incredible intelligence. Their intelligence and ours collided together, in an unrelenting breach of sanity, like matter and anti-matter instantly annihilating each other.

Unbeknownst to the rest of human civilization, a war raged for control of Europa. The indigenous life there, tens of millions of years older than ourselves, were driving us, the invaders, back. Millions of humans and Europans were killed. I was the leader of that force against them. Earth was dying, both Luna and Mars were destroyed, and Europa was the last place in the solar system where humanity had a chance for survival. I was on the mission of the ages to save the human race. I had no choice. I was helpless. I was our last hope for survival and the savior of humanity, or so they told me.

I was wanted by the Europans and was captured by them, who examined me, put me through many tests, and tortures for my genocidal mania. They sought to learn all they could about humans and did not care about what they were doing to me, pain and torture were not a part of their lexicon. And they had only the goal to learn how to kill their enemy in the most efficient way possible, and to punish me as a one representative for the sins of the entire species.

As a final punishment, they sent me to the Oblivion complex on Triton. Since the complex did not exist in their time because of the time dilation while traveling at speed, I was sent away in space, and in time, to be forever forgotten, and forever ignored. I always assumed that the place was a mining installation. I assumed it was made by *humans*! It was not at all! The Europans gave me false memories and knowledge to make me believe whatever they wanted me to believe.

I expected none of the reality before me. I was the one who was charged with the murdering of them all in the name of manifest destiny. I was the monster. I was the evil one. I am the mad man. I was the destroyer of worlds. But I also tried to make peace. It failed.

~

"You are in expectation of nothing," the Europan replied. "We are in expectation of something. Your worlds are dead."

Then I was shown the final assault on humanity, or at least what they wanted me to see as that. The Europans, far in advancement of us evolutionarily, finally decided that enough was enough. They had developed abilities to think things into reality, just by *thinking* them. They were normally a benevolent and loving species, who wished no harm to any form of life, but had observed through the eons, the rise of humanity, its painful incline to sentience, its advancement in technology, its initial explorations followed by its rise to power in the solar system, and its insistent retention of selfish, irrational greed, power, exploitation, and violence. They viewed us as vermin, how we view rats, disgusting creatures, cancer, for which no favor could be granted, and for which there was no cure. When we tried to colonize their home world, it was we who were the alien invaders.

They wished no co-existence. They wished no peace. We were the rats to them. We were the cockroaches to them. We were Ebola to them. We were SARS to them. Then, in an instant of united thought formed by a mastery of the Creative force in every living being, they wished us out of existence by their thought that created it. And then all living humans in that instant were simply wiped from existence as if they never been before.

Except for me.

I, was completely and utterly...

...alone.

~

Not the kind of alone where you might be in a room alone and there are others in another room, or in another building, or in another town. Not like that. This was completely different. I was desolately alone in that humanity never existed. There were no other humans because humans never existed. I would *never* see another human face. And in letting that sink in, I realized I would see only mine, which was worse than seeing none at all. The Europans altered the universe with a single thought that removed all of humanity and then in another removed me from that, and I was moved from the version of it that contained humanity in any way.

It was truly, Oblivion. True. Cold. Oblivion.

I was spiritually obliterated. The memory placed in my mind was that at the very moment Europa thought humanity away, I was cryo-frozen in a prison-ship and sent to Neptune at three-quarters the speed of light.

But the fact there was still a pile of corpse on Triton when I arrived still puzzled me. So, I asked. After all, what did I truly have to lose?

"Who are all the others of my kind in this time that were here in that pile?"

"They are there. They are no one." And the creature pointed to the pile of bodies at the spiked wall, which itself was two rooms behind me, but there they were, nonetheless, at least in my perception of them.

"And so, what, for me? Will there be torture later? If so, I'll need a drink. A stiff one. Maybe 37. And where's the cot? No jail cells? No work details? And like what, eighty people? What bullshit is this?"

"You will be shown. Yes. Unknown. No. No. Yes. Unknown. Restate."

"I do not understand." I responded.

"Look at them again." It insisted.

I was then accelerated toward the pile of bodies.

"Look upon their faces." It forced my head directly in front of the bloodied, bashed flesh that was the putrid pile of effervescing rotting meat, mere centimeters away from my nostrils. The smell of it rank and beyond description.

I looked, closely, as I was forced to. The light was dim, to the extreme. The Europan pushed my head closer and closer.

Closed eyes then opened, suddenly, and faces then became, mine.

"Look upon all that you are, vermin!" The creature exclaimed. "You are the scourge of existence, and the giver of pain. You see nothing but yourself in everything. You are the selfish virus feeding off the lives all around you. You are the rotting corpses you see before you. You are all that they were! They. Are. You!"

I lay on the ground, shaking, beaten, and overpowered. The faces morphed and twisted into likenesses of my own, and slowly I came to know that they were indeed all my own. Then I could see only faces around me. The faces! Oh Lord, help me! The faces were all around me, like zombies of myself, staring into my soul, in the red light, shining on their corpses. All me at the end of various journeys through lives and lessons. All designed to end up here, in this place, this prison for my soul.

I then appeared still in the red chair, a part of it, saw the walls close in and white protuberances come towards me, form sharp hooks and spikes. The came upon me, penetrated my flesh and ripped it off my bones, slowly, agonizingly...I writhed and screamed in agony. And then all went black.

I awoke in the pile of corpses and rank putrescence. Hot CO2 rose from the pile I had become a part of and penetrated the cooler ambient air around me. Then, in an instantaneous flash I was back at the point of realization and my awareness and remembering of my crimes, and the same process, occurred and I experienced the pain and agony of a thousand million lives crying out for mercy with every tear of my bloodied, useless flesh, only to wake once again at the moment of realization that I committed genocide, and as my punishment, the Europans cured the solar system of the human virus, saving me as its one, last example.

Time had no meaning here. I didn't know how many more times I endured the repeating, circular agonies. I had only recollections of the very beginning and the very end for an instant then unending pain, and spiritual torture. How many times? A hundred, a thousand, a quadrillion? Stubborn creature I was. Oblivion was upon me and suddenly, after the quadrillion and fifth time (or the third, I cannot be sure), I knew pure...*agony*, and I was enlightened.

~

Then the great lesson finally was upon me. The white room. The faceless people. They were also all me. I was all of them. *All* of them! There were never any other humans! It was only me all along! All my lives that made me, all of me was there! Every life I ever lived to that point ended in this place; this Oblivion place, a spiritual nexus for the soul, a vinculum of reincarnation. In other words, hell.

"I must get back!" I shouted. In my mind I realized that since time had no meaning I could go whenever I wanted to make a different choice. To the faceless people and the red button. If I was right, I could help them make—*think!*—a different choice.

"I need to be back there!" I yelled out, and just as the sandwich, the shoes, and the flashlight appeared before my eyes, and just as I was instantaneously transported to the room with the chair, and then was I accelerated to white room.

The fourteen remaining faceless people were still there, to my surprise, making their staircase. I was in the middle of them.

"Make a different choice, assholes!" I exclaimed to the faceless robotic automaton versions of me doomed to repeat the same mistake again and again. One by one I forced each of them to step on the same red button as before. At the first step, and then one by one thereafter, the tortured memories of my previous actions faded from my memory, and my *reality,* whatever that meant in *this* place. Finally, I came to the last of them, to myself. We came close together, our bodies slowly merging together in a grand light, in a union of souls, forgetful souls, and became one. I hit the red button on the floor with *my* foot and was catapulted through all the past lives I had lived. A relived them and experienced them as if being told stories through their eyes. They were in front of me, like doors in a long hallway, like a grand tall theatre, stacked high and wide. I somehow knew to choose one to return to the life most fulfilling to me, apart from the destroyer of worlds, and I knew, somehow, I could escape Oblivion.

How I knew any of this was a mystery. Perhaps I always knew it and the Europans were testing me like before. Maybe they planted the thought in my head, as if painting on an empty canvas. Perhaps the entire cavalcade of torturous events that I endured was not them torturing me, but *me* torturing me. Maybe the Europans' final punishment was to have the criminal gaze into the mirror, a spiritual mirror, and forced him to look hard at the ugliest parts of itself.

Maybe there were no Europans at all and I was sick with a fever and I was delusional. Bah!

I became then, what I am then, or what I was, before, the writer, like before, in my head, in another life. I was the creator of new worlds, new concepts and new lessons. I became enlightened and became the creator within the cosmos I create. I exist because of the cosmos, and the cosmos in my mind exists because of me. And becomes therefore part of the greater cosmos because of the creative force within me that added to it. The infinite numbers of imaginative places I created in my own mind, become the cosmos that I perceive, in reality. I give the cosmos the depth, complexity, and existence I need to stay sane, and in return, the Creator gives me the Gift of the creative force that I glean from the vectors of infinities all around me. I am the reader. I am the writer, the creator of worlds! Timeless.

~

I found myself back in a transport ship looking at the view screen. No door was opened where none had been before. I gazed at the myriad ships departing and docking at Europa station. Human ships. Human. There were no Europans except for some cyanobacteria found by some thermal vents at Octavia Mons. No nine-foot tall Europans within a light year were to be found. Maybe I would meet one in 100 million years as evolved, sentient creatures on their own, so they can find me and pay me my fate that was Oblivion. But for now, my experience on Triton was but memory, a dream, a nightmare, or maybe it was my soul truly in the hell I made for it in some future life existence.

I got that stiff drink.

"Maybe I will make Triton the subject of my latest novel." I put down the glass of bourbon I was holding. I was about to meet with my agent anyway, and the landing cycle had just commenced.

VIII

Light

I lose no souls to you for I am the place where all souls reside.

December 99, 9999. 99:99 c^2 am

I had remembered a bed, and the warm touch of a woman (*Jessica!*) in a previous life, but my nightmare was still as intense as ever. I sought the experience of a wiser force, one who was an older soul than I, who knew the ways of human interaction, foreknowledge, and wisdom. I spoke with him candidly but always, always never letting him see the whole me. I questioned that action and came to realize that perhaps what I was trying to protect was nothing but the will to be independent from all else—to remain "objective." The darker side of my soul I was not yet ready to be unleashed—to be free. And by that I felt that I, myself was not yet ready to be free, perhaps unconsciously.

With this new tormentor, this mentor, this wise old soul, I spoke of perspective, objectivity, of things entitled, "big pictures," and of light. We spoke of how such things were so easy for me to see, and how others in my circle were so less enlightened than I, that it was difficult to tolerate their ignominious recklessness in my mind. I, therefore, explained of how I was once accused of not seeing this "big picture" by the tormenting soul from which there was no escape until I laid claim to my victory over her in my mind. The tormentor, my boss in my nightmare, persisted to degrade my being in making me believe that I could, and never would, be anything more than she.

I wanted to say in response to her pushing my face into the dark, wet soil with the soul of her foot that the picture I saw made theirs the size of a muon in the heart of my mind. I wanted to say that the insignificance of all that was immediately around me stood below me as I intellectually connected point to point in space and time. I wanted to say that the light of the world is the light of every soul's energy combined and fused into a vast super-consciousness that is the realm in which God exists. God the Creator and the Cosmos itself were both living things born from the fount of creation. Perhaps they were one and the same.

If the light of the physical world and the Light of the spirit were indeed the same, then I could say thus that whatever dark there is in the

Cosmos, there will always be a measure of light. And no matter how dark, the light travels through it. The dark has no power. It is its absence. I wanted to crush her again with my mind. I enjoyed fixating upon it, and repeating, repeating, repeating. I told the old soul who was my guide these things.

He grinned and nodded affirmatively, like they do with his other mental patients.

Though he was wise, he was but still green to my vast observances. I could not come close to conveying in words all the worlds and the places I experienced—I *lived.* I wish that someone would see the light and *Light* as I do. I wish I could say that it was like that.

The nightmare had suddenly passed a little to the left of time, as it melted, dripping slowly like mayonnaise from the corset of existence, wound tight, slowly releasing the circulation of that which was wholly constricted. I could not fathom an existence of pure, otiose, belaboring anti-creation, summoned here to simply "...highlight all the 'M's. To leave nothing for anyone else who would not know, or care of my existence here plagued me at nightmare's end.

The maddening noise of the unrelenting dripping, clicking clock's drips finally ran out of the fluid, that was the bottle of time that fueled it.

I had once come from the light and into the light, as a creature of great strength and of great lesson. And great promise. But this world immersed me, steeped me, into maddening antilogic, anti-reason, and inside a crucible of neither point nor purpose nor personification that meant a damn to anyone. I exist. Therefore, nothing.

There was the lesson of reflection, philosophizing on what made humanity work best, worst, why it destroyed everything it created by annihilating the one thing that made it great (*creation!*) only to rise great civilizations and then just to be burnt to ash by mobs of animals who felt the power of complaint as justification to destroy.

But, alas, I could not tell you what the specifics were now. Am I the dramatic one? Where did that come from? I know not what you think, so don't expect more than what you communicate. I care not to read your pathetic little minds and explore the cosmos within which I see as the grain's grain of sand on a vast African desert and savannah with pride in my Pride during a hot, dry spell in the anticlimax of a monsoon never formed (*insanity!*). I become what I wish to learn. Hence, there will be no other way to learn better than being that which is learned itself.

I then become the light, within the light. Light is the energy of all the souls of the cosmos that push the cosmos ever further from itself, in a sojourn of sorts—without the blinks of any eyes. Light is the creative force, for all things are reduced to light in its simplest form...something about all matter being interchangeable with energy some madman shared with the world once.

Einstein, a man of great vision but of poor confidence, proved that light itself moves time. Light, as the cosmos's constant, pushes and pulls at time as its motion is perceived by all the souls of the cosmos. Matter and energy then compare the motion of light to their own motion, and that is how all the souls in the cosmos measure time, as a function of relativity. Time then is the fluid variable, that drips at differing rates, that can be a variably viscous force that, to my unending chagrin, my species has decided to measure all events by. Unfortunately, no one has yet made the connection to the realm of truth and power—no one yet, until now.

We are all creatures of light. The cosmos is made of light. It was first light, and nothing else. In the primordial atom that burst forth with all the information that created the entire, vast cosmos, that information was transmitted through an infinitesimal point that only energy could pass through. Although the cosmos lost energy and transformed pure light into particles of matter, which is simply the difference between kinetic and potential energy states, which formed the chemicals that make us, we are still all light. Everything is light, just in different states, just as ice and steam are still water made of H2O but act and appear completely differently.

Perhaps light itself has many states and the particle soup we swim in is the result of its properties as differing, innumerable states, infinitely more complex than the quadrillion synapses connected in the human brain, and therefore, can be considered conscious.

My guide was above me, and he placed a device on my skull, a gag in my mouth, and strapped my arms and legs down to the bed. And after he said, “Nurse, when I say, go ahead and start the procedure.”

“Yes doctor,” she replied flatly.

I jolt ripped through my body and skull and the world went from being dim and incoherent to a blinding white light that was all around me. All that was real in the cosmos was stripped away from me and I was shown, my guide had shown me, my divine, watchful, wonderful guide, that the cosmos was full of light, was all light, that I was *all light*!

I then felt warmth through my body, and the light faded again back to the grey underpinnings of the desolate realm I inhabited in my nightmare. “Doctor,” the nurse began, “I’m ready for number two.”

“Okay...vitals look good, seizure is in control. He’s coming out of it. Okay. I’ll say when...”

And the flash of divine universal truth flowed over me like a warm blanket on a winters’ cold day where the wind bites at your marrow in a way that it inescapable. The beauty of white, unending, infinite light was overwhelming. I sobbed in my soul at its beauty. And I thought to myself that this is what heaven must be like.

I considered also then that the carbon atom can bond on four sides, with almost any other atom. Is this by accident, at random, a coincidence? Perhaps. But perhaps not. Carbon then has the unique ability in practically any state to create complex amino acids, the building-blocks of life itself—the cosmos begets—creates—itself. For it to exist, the cosmos must be perceived by an observer or group of observers, or by groups of observers, or by groups of groups of observers, and so on. The maddening circular reasoning was upon me again and the light disappeared as quickly as it appeared. I wailed in the dim.

I heard the nurse say, "His pulse is up to 173, doctor."

The doctor responded, "Okay. Looks like we'll have to go again. Shit. It's already 5:30 and I really didn't want to miss the Babe today. Oh well," he said in a long drone that he seemed to say okay in, like saying, "oh...kay..." slowly, like an exhale after the best night ever. The dim rank air was around me. And my thoughts in clarity—*confusion!*—returned.

Again, we then can now say that if an observer can perceive an object or event, then that object or event must exist because that perception is within the cosmos that created it—the Cosmos, Creator, God—the living God all around us, all at once, everywhere. I yelled as loud as I could, “God created us, and I observe what he created and if there was no one to see what He created, then what he created does not exist because there’s no one here to say so, so there’s no here, here, in here out there, that is in only in here....” I trailed off.

Unfortunately for my guide, and to my chagrin and unending disdain, all he could perceive was mild grunting and the drool pooling in the vinyl cushion and dripping slowly on the floor.

“Ready doctor?” the nurse asked.

“Yes, I believe so. Pulse is 134. O2 looks good. Okay. Last one. Three...two...one.”

Let there be Light.

So then, the nightmare truly ended, and I was back in the guff with the souls I had bonded with in my previous lives. I was in joy, as were they. I, and them, as existing only as Light—without form and without concept of time—existed only to enlighten one another. I happily immersed myself into the warm waters of eternal enlightenment. The Creator, the one who exists always from all perspectives all at once, gave us His love and renewed our souls, and prepared us for the next lesson—a soul’s lesson—in a new life, with a new breath, in a new shell.

The dripping brain-poison that is the destroyer of souls that says perception constructs reality was wholly destroyed, in that moment. I saw clearly with the crystalline exactness of light rays that objective reality existed, and what I perceive of it is wholly irrelevant to, and within, the cosmos. And I knew that I existed. Therefore, I must exist!

...And the cosmos sighed,

...and shrugged.

Then, another moment came.

The dim haze from the comfort of my cell was interrupted by a crazy person who somebody forced me to sit next to. I was screaming at the orderlies to get the animal away from me and that her smell made me want to regurgitate all over the floor. I explained who I was and that no one should be treated like animals as they treat me. I was, after all, the head of the science department of Cambridge University, and was there for 34 years until the middle of the Great War. I explained myself crisply and clearly, so that there would be no misunderstanding. I endeavored to remain as respectful and dignified as possible while I was in hospital. I certainly would not want my reputation to be tarnished because of my treatment.

My temples ached and burned from the electrodes that burned the skin that was my only barrier to this accursed, outside world. But, alas, the others simply smiled and nodded agreeably like they always did.

I could not perceive that in their dull cow-eyed disinterest, they could only understand the slow, exhaling, expelling gasp of a stunted grunt that accompanied my tilted head that allowed the warm saliva, that was my beloved, dripping drool, to land on the arm of my wheel chair, while I gazed at pigeon droppings that were slowly, but inexorably, being washed by a steady rain on the gray concrete, profoundly catatonic, staring out the window, as the most profound realization of my life.

IX

Sojourns

I lose myself to you for I am the one who vanquishes the "me" to understand the "you."

December 00, 0000, 0:00am

Light. There was only light!

I immerged from the euphoric, blinding light that was as white as the purest, cleanest snow, adrift on a cool ocean current, miles high above the earth. Puffy cumulus clouds kept me company as I drifted through the clear air. Below me was blue, deep cobalt blue, and above, blue. Deep cobalt blue. In front, behind, an all around me a fading lightening of still more blue that was like a ribbon of mist, demarking the boundary of blue and blue, one above and one, below.

As I rose toward the blue above me, the temperature cooled, and then the opposite, the opposite. I felt the change upward as the white bright sun rose higher in the sky and later, made the sky pink and orange, as though it were a storage, for vast feast of infinite color within its massive gape. When the light dimmed in the natural, recurring cycle that was the day, I floated downward toward the other blue, replete with dancing white dashes on its skin, forever in motion. Then to be lifted skyward again when the warmth of the air below would blow me back up to sky's divine purity, unspoiled by anything that may have been swimming (or crawling) below.

Before long, I came upon a butterfly riding the same stream of air with me. He greeted me in the usual way, by holding steadfastly resolute to its course, barely aware of my existence.

"Hello friend!" I called out.

He turned, startled, surprised to suddenly be engaged in a discussion in this most unlikely of situations. "I great you! You are greeted." He called back.

"I'm Justin," I replied. "I'm finding my home, so I can settle down and put down roots."

"Ah," he said in kind, "Isn't that a coincidence! My name is Justin too!"

We both snickered slightly at the uncanny coincidence as a fresh blast of changing air moved us both slightly southward. Justin then asked, "Oh? Where are you heling from?"

I thought briefly, searching my small memory for an answer. I could only think of and say to my companion, "The light."

"The Light? Huh. I don't understand." Justin said to me. I thought a bit more about the brief flashes of memory pictures in my conscience and I recalled an image of a vast grassy plain in a warm solid place that was home to a pride. "I remember a savanna." I said further.

"Oh. Okay." Butterfly Justin changed the subject. "I just got my wings dry finally after struggling to climb a tree this morning and had to get through a sticky, nasty spider's web."

"What?" I asked incoherently. "Morning? Spider's web? What's that?"

Justin laughed at me and began to turn further south, away from my drifting course. "Never mind, namesake! Well, this is my turn. Good luck to you! I am off to the large land in the south!" I turned and watched him turning south, and in the corner of my eye I was witness to hundreds of orange and black butterflies that dotted the blue heaven behind my new friend, Justin. Monarchs, the word burst in my mind.

"What's land?" I muttered to myself.

They say if you travel far enough in the cosmos you eventually meet yourself. In the far distance on another cycle that was far removed from my chance meeting with another cosmic observer, I saw a in the pale blue demarking haze and strip of a new color: brown, in the far-off distance. I felt a kinship to it as it was the same color as myself.

Brown. The color of home. The color of the foundation. Where I shall put down roots and grow. For, there is no finer goal in life. That is, when you are rooted, your life has purpose, it grows and prospers with others of your kind beside you who only want to be grounded and grow, as yourself, reaching for your own grand end. There may be ongoing competition to reach the light, but invariably, we all manage have what we need to thrive. No one needs to provide it as a resource because the light, itself is the source of all growth. It is the energy by which provides the engines of my world, inside of me.

The earth grounds me, keeps me stolid, resolute and anchored still so I may grow into a deep, far reaching cosmic observer. The brown, good earth provides the food I need to use the energy the light provides so I am best able to transform into new and unforeseen heights and perspectives. Without the ground, I would starve! I would be floating, without a direction to grow, without perspective on life, as it would always be blue, and I would surely lose myself, or be lost to the winds that carry me now.

The shadows and darkness, conversely, divides and breaks down a being. It steals its energy, stunts its growth and makes rotten its very core. The dark of the winter cold stunts all growth, it kills all movement, all energy is sapped and removed so that nothing can evolve. In the light of the summer do all things flourish, when properly grounded at their base, in the good brown earth.

The land was getting closer an I felt the stream of air pushing me ever closer.

"Soon! Soon," I exclaimed, "Soon I will be home. Finally, home!" No one could hear me of course as my namesake was long away from me, and for all I knew I was the only cosmic observer left in the entire blue cosmos that was all around me.

To the north, I observed a new structure in the purely smooth blue sphere that wrapped me. It was long and round, puffy, and white. Some parts were gray, more toward the paler blue line that divided the sky from the sea. I looked again, and it was bigger, and grayer. I looked again, and it spread over half the blue above me. I looked again, and all the blue was gone, everywhere. And all became gray.

Beneath me now the brown land was racing towards me at incredible speed. The wind that carried me suddenly calmed and then stood up again, in whirling, chaotic directions. I felt me being lurched around, back and forth, up and down, until I had no way of knowing which way was up, which was straight, and what was right. The chaos of the tumult that came with the gray wind had taken all direction from me, so that I panicked and writhed for control of anything to rectify my plight.

It grew darker, when I noticed, and then it was wet. Spheres of water flew around me and at me from all directions and hit me so hard that it jolted me in to even greater chaos. Most were liquid, but some were also solid, and when they pelted me, I became stunned, disoriented and defeated. I was at the mercy of the storm, the storm of chaos and thunder and flashed of light that pushed me down toward the earth. It pushed me, forced me to be away from the light, and away from the clear air. It was trying to defeat me, to erase me, to shove me into a place I did not wish to go.

Yet the good earth was still racing upward toward me and the tumultuous water pelts were falling and pulling me towards it as I became soaked and heavy by its presence. Before long the white mist that was the cosmos around me gave way to the brown earth that was dotted with orange and brown, and green, and gold. The brown earth was made up of these colors and before long, I saw that most of the good earth was not brown at all, but those colors and more.

"Red!" I shouted.

I saw it for the first time as pieces of it whizzed by at incredible speed. I gave myself permission to forget the chaos ensuing around me and allowed my gaze to focus and become rooted in this great discovery. After all, how can a color be described if it has never been seen before?

I dropped. Landed. Earthbound. Home.

There was dark, water, soil, and things were cool. There was a hiss all around me of tall things that swayed in the wind of the graying cosmos around me. I dimmed. The light dimmed. Then all became dark.

Another cycle had begun, and the light had returned! I was beneath great and tall specimens of me that were mostly dark gray and without colors at their tips. The tumultuous chaos must have blown them off in the gray from before. I was wet and dirty, and I felt myself sinking into the good earth, and fatigue grabbed me. There was call to sleep. The dark and the cold called me to sleep, whereas the light and the warmth call me to wake. The dark called me to sleep. And the sleep crept on me like a thick sap driving slowly down an unsuspecting trunk.

In my dreamy slumber, the thought of being in control over my landscape, I thought of sojourns through different perceptions—my endless lives as independent, but true realities—as what I had come to understand as my being the free soul, the cosmic observer, free to explore the infinite sojourns of stories and lessons and record them for all time. If I could be blessed to continue, the being I was before would be inexorably changed and evolved so that I could be closer to the Creator—would understand far more than the person of old. I would vanquish the "me" to understand the "you"—and the One.

My dreamscape played inside me, and I saw myself walking into an office, the new tormenting soul's place of business and source of all my torment and anguish, prepared to fully illustrate to him that I had evolved. I screamed inside myself that I was a far greater mind than he had any perception of, and that others of my kind—us cosmic observers—must be recognized, vindicated and celebrated! I was prepared to tell him of my visits to many grand places, in great unfathomable times, and how those times—those lives! —all had led me to the life as a writer, and a publisher had accepted to take the plunge, and risk an investment on me, who to them was an "unknown" author.

But they led with their faith and their belief. They were grounded in their resolute intrepid explorers' mission to create new worlds, new dreams in stories, and tell them to as many who would listen. And because of that, they trusted my work; they trusted me. They had the faith to pursue and communicate to the world this grand new perspective on the nature of the cosmos, and our role in it—and the cosmos returned to me what I so yearned to be given: credibility among all. And with that gift, I was...forever... *vindicated*!

Upon my telling him this, he finally—*finally!* —understood the scope of my understanding. The way in which I perceived the cosmos, the need for the One to exist, regardless of physical laws, the reflective nature of the cosmos itself, the reward for perseverance, and the inferred punishment for doing harm. I projected unto him the vast expanse of the cosmos and permitted myself to feel glad for my achievement. No other soul would ever again be able to torment me again. The faith I had gained in myself, through the independent resolute introspective mind that experienced the cosmos in so many ways, through that success did I complete my conquest of the tormenting souls that pursued me in them all.

I learned that I needed to be what the cosmos shaped my soul to become, and what most fulfilled my soul. It was not quite destiny, but a specific predisposition to like or dislike certain activities, and actions, thus steering me in a certain direction and certain purpose. My agenda felt completed, and hence, my actions were as close to pure as a human being could get to. I was glad and proud of my accomplishment. Others in my nightmare—my dream—were proud as well. I was respected and legitimized through that respect. I rested my work badge on her table and my last words to him were, "And to you I leave your perception of me. Handle it with care."

I exited into the light of a brightened dream—the vast light of only good and purity. I wrote as I walked far above the landscape which melted below my feet. Clouds in my eyes were rapidly whizzing by, and their color allowed my mind to open to their beauty. Souls were all around me and I felt their warmth, and their goodness.

"Was this death?" I asked to myself aloud. I was not sure where I was or why. I saw before me the same as what was behind me, above me, and below me. I melted into my own thoughts, and bright amber glowing rocks floated before me in the air I needed not breathe. I was aware of all things, at all times, all thoughts, of all observers, all at once. I again wrote what was there. The sky below me winked in and out of existence as their starts created their own fortunes in a roulette wheel of dripping time. I wanted not for hunger and I yearned not for pain. There was no feeling, but fully, the feeling that was, where I was, became my domain, my destination, and the beginning of the ending of my journey, all in the one moment that it was intended, that yielded the infinite domain, that was my grand end.

Warmth!

Light!

Wet!

My slumber was vanquished! And suddenly, my being rose from the inky blackness of the dark and cold, the divider, the destroyer of all good things, the stopper of all movement, and was pushed back and away so that the engines of the cosmos could be reconnected to my very being. Those engines, containing infinite energies, the very fount of the creative force, created within me the purpose of all life: to grow, to live, to thrive. I burst. And from two ends the means to my enduring existence went forth and conquered. The cosmos had gifted me with the means to transcend the seed of life I was before into this new vision of the future, in the husk of an old, box of potential, to objective, actual reality.

I came to lay down roots and roots I did lay! Deeper and deeper, wider and wider did they spread in the moist spring soil that was the meltwater slurry of nutrient-rich food that was my lifeline to the future. Those were below. Above, another tendril rose and from it did I fan out to collect the pure, white light. The light that adds and multiplies all good things in the cosmos, was for me, the engine of the world. And in the spring, that engine did start.

I looked, and a six-legged creature walked past me.

"Good day to you sir!" He said as I stood stolidly in his presence.

"Good day!" I replied. "The light is wonderful this day, warm and bright!"

"Indeed, it is!" He said in return. "I'm Yeshua. You are...new here I take it?"

"I am. Please to meet you. I'm...I'm...hmm. I don't seem to know."

"You'll know, soon." the ant said as he smiled at me and walked past. "You'll know when you know. You will know!"

I didn't know what he meant by that, but it was clear that if I was going to put down roots here, that I would need to figure out how others would address me. I was just a newcomer in a strange land, and I would need to earn my place if I am expected to thrive and be respected by all others. Then when all went black for an instant, and something crushed me, the weight of the whole earth on top of me.

"Hey!" I shouted. "Watch where you're walking!" I large, fury bear, brown and with smaller versions of itself accompanying it simply turned, looked at my crushed self, and snorted, its breath creating two jets of mist in the air that looked like the clouds that pelted water upon me in the blue universe I arrived from. The pain of the impact took many cycles to rid itself of me.

The sun returned, and I stretched with all my might to reach for the white, for the blue, for the light that was the good, that was the divine muse of creation that pushed me to advance, to survive, to thrive. In the dark I retreated, I rested, I used the time (whatever that even meant) to repair my damages and to store energy from the good brown earth. Having a solid foundation was the surest way to grow, in all things.

What's in a name? Supposing that if it means something to someone else, whom you never met before, then you could acquire their meaning of it for yourself and build your life around that. But deep down, thing of this, it made me feel like a cheat—that I was taking an easy way toward self-value through the appropriation of someone else's meaning and value in a name. Those who are named haven't a choice, and they're stuck with whatever irrational abhorrent constructs drug-crazed creatures place on their offspring.

But in making a name for oneself, the name is just a word. The value of the word is to others based on the deeds associated with cosmic observer they achieve in their time and become memorable. For me, my value is in my perseverance to hold fast to my mission, to put down roots and grow, thrive and prosper. To be the tallest of them all, is my mission. And I'll not let anything stand in my way and block the pure, good light if at all I can help it. Words are just words. The meaning behind them are based on actions, deeds, achievements, abhorrent acts, or infamousness. Choose your deeds, and your name will be, your *name.*

Many cycles passed, and I remained stolid, resolute. I became strong, and before long no creature on the good brown earth trampled me or pressed me into the ground any more. Other starters tried to steal my good, pure light, and they failed. The failed because me breadth and my height were wider and bigger than all else in the space, and they could not collect the good light from me. I claimed my domain. And I earned my place among my cousins.

As I grew my cousins would speak of the word from the vine. News travels fast when connected to the forest. Messages delivered on the wind or in the root come almost instantly from faraway places, that I arrived, and that I had taken root! Another message came too, a new wave of concern and ponder, a group known as humans were rising in the west, and with them came only destruction by axe and fire. Whole sections of forest were being cut away as they spread and advanced, like lichen across stone, or the natural rising and falling of the seas.

Information was silent but full of voice, deep with color, rich with description, and replete with vibrancy. There was no grapevine effect because information on the wind, chemically, was the same, no matter how close or how far it originated. If in root, then it was all connected, interlinked, and instantaneous perfect information. Humans were rising, and building, and infesting.

After 365 thousand cycles, humans were everywhere, destroying everything green and alive but also building immense structures that towered into the sky taller even than I! They travelled the seas, rode over land, flew in the air, traveled beyond to earth's partner in orbit high above, an even to other worlds. They were incredible creatures. They lived in a relative instant but were capable of so much! I listened intently to the wind each cycle for the latest adventurous news of the day.

Before long, my excitement was replaced by disappointment and fear. Their blight on the word spread so far that my brethren were being cut, brothers and sisters 300 paces high and hundreds of thousands of cycles old put down in a relative instant, never to be seen again. The piled their waste everywhere; their waste formed an island in the western sea as big as a continent! They made poison from their need for more energy. Before long they built nothing new but struggled to keep what had been built. Their great population centers began to crumble, their people multiplied and multiplied.

They starved. Diseases rose to meet them as evolution struggled to stem the tide their instantaneous cancerous overpopulation. They called them flu, tuberculosis, hepatitis, Ebola, Aids, SARS, and other strange words that the wind could not decipher. They were mammals, but acted as viruses, as animals, and had no purpose before long other than to consume one another in an orgy of cannibalistic engorgement.

Then there was the great fire. Not the fires I yearn for to drop and spread my cones. No, this fire was of a flame that burned as the sun. It was so hot that when it dissipated all that lived still got burned. Great towers of flame rose into the clear blue sky above and made black the pure water below. It was the flame that would always burn, save for the cleansing waters that would come in response to it.

The great flood ingulfed much of the land. Many parts of the forest were lost in those cycles, and information was disrupted. The human animal lingered, and slowly fell. Try as they might to build and advance, so they flew, they still fought and, once again they regressed into the chaos and tumult that was their nature. I was as tall as a mountain! And I would not be fell by a mere movement of water or a rambling band of club-swinging animals.

After more than a million cycles, their fires and deafening wail were gone from the earth, and yet I stood; yet I remained. I had grown tall and stout, in both stature and awareness, and had become the largest in my group. In the insanity of the mob that was humanity, a ray of reason came from them that pierced through wailing noise they made like a needle penetrating to the center of a boil, and they preserved a tiny area of the good, brown earth that I stood, protected from their destruction. And in that moment of clarity and reason, they left me one thing though that I could not bring myself to provide, nor could it be provided save for my deeds by any other. On the smallest strip of land, they preserved, and in front of me, they placed a sign, and on that sign, they gave me a name:

Giant Sequoia.

I had become a giant among trees, among species, among life, and among the events of the world, and I was named for it. And I felt great. I stood for eons and saw the greatest and worst of the world and that could evolve from it. Objective. Strong. Stoic. I was the stolid resolute. I had put down roots and held my ground.

I was the stolid resolute.

I did not sway in the wind.

I was the stolid resolute.

I was the strength of the base of the trunk.

I was the stolid resolute.

And I, finally, had a name.

The darkness came after 130 more cycles as it always did, and I rested and enjoyed my slumber most this time, as the world was free from the problems of everything associated with the mob of club-wielding barbarians, their fires and machines. They said they wanted to save the world. But the world needed saving from them. And the world, evolution, nature herself corrected the problem as she always did and rid her of the disease that infested her body. She culled the infestation and the smart ones left for new worlds in a grand migration that was a sight to behold.

Before long after the silence had finally come, I rested, and in the dark, in the cold, in the still, I weakened and slumbered, never to wake or to see the clear blue sky or pure white light at this height, again. And again, before long, the light came for me once more.

~

The light came and stayed, dimmed and flashed like a strobe. Like a blind in my mind, suddenly, and all was again a distant fuzz of perception. A ringing stirred my senses and I alone could hear what I heard. It persisted. I raised my lids to reveal a water-stained ceiling, and heavy blanketed coverings over my nude body.

I woke. After a night of restless sleep, I was none to be sure but only to agree. I felt as if the room spun with my every lid flex. Not remembering much, but knowing I had dreamt something, I was reminded by the banging in my head that the phone was buzzing. I reached over to answer it in the darkened bedroom.

"Justin. You still napping?" It was my wife, Jessica.

"Uh. Yeah. I guess I just woke up. What time is it?" It was dark outside, and I heard the city traffic in the streets below.

"5:30 or so. You slept all afternoon my sicky-hubby-boo? How do you feel?"

"Ugh. Stop. Okay, I guess. Still hot. I must still have the fever." I rose from my sweat-soaked bed the smelled of rank putrescence that was strangely sweet.

"You're really sick hon. We'll check your temperature when I get home. You want me to pick up some medicine or anything?"

"Yeah. Good. Medicine. Advil. Some ginger ale would be good too."

"Okay. I'll even cook for you. How does that sound?"

"Mm." She was a horrible cook. But at that point, who was I to argue?

"Okay. I'll be home in about a half-hour."

"That's fine." A pause. "I love you, Jes."

"I love you too, Jus. Feel better. I'll be home soon."

"Yeah. Smooch." I hung up the phone and stared at the planes flying overhead making their way from the airport which I knew was just behind the highway off in the distance. Then I stared beyond them and saw in my mind a butterfly making its way up a Giant Sequoia, whose poor, little body and wings were water-soaked, and the chap was struggling to get dry. I saw an image of a canopy of trees below me and I being the tallest, and greatest, tree around, rising above the tumult of the world below.

"As big as a mountain!" I muttered to myself. I suddenly had an urge to write down what I saw, and maybe even begin a new novel. I sat at the side of the bed, still looking out the window. The blanket around my body I wrapped tighter as I shivered in the heat of my own body's biological reaction to the influenza virus. The city lights illuminated the fog and it all looked as if it were a movie set, not quite real, not quite right, and not quite there–kind of *un*-there.

Something beyond and within me had definitely, and inevitably,

...

...changed.

The End

Epilogue

In writing this multilayer, juxtaposed and metaphorical novel, I discovered many areas of imagination and logic within myself that I knew nothing about before. For that, I am thankful. The limitless expectations of my own imagination created the previous pages, and I, now more than ever, as a cosmic observer, a recorder, a communicator, and as a human being, have hopefully shown and opened many doors for interested readers.

Do not be afraid to look at your own perceptions of what is written herein. And most importantly, do not be limited by my perception of my own sojourns. Embellish all that there is to embellish and create all that there is to be created. Believe in the truth of your own imagination. And certainly, believe that nothing in your cosmos can be unreal, for if you imagine it, it must exist for you. I agree with Plato, when he said, "a wise man is one who has something to say, a fool, one who must say something." We all have something important to *say*. Find it and say it. Do not ever be placed into a position where you have to say *something*. One is proactive, the other, reactive. Be proactively communicative. Never be anyone but yourself; be who the cosmos lets you become and has gifted to you the tools to make it happen within your own spirit to know right from wrong, good from evil, reason from tumult. Be the stolid resolute, and the silent introspect.

Look for deeper meaning in the words, the metaphors, and themes, because there's more a book than its cover. Find the center, the compass, the pure white light. Reach for it. Overcome the fear of the unknown. Jump out of a plane and land in another plain of reality more bizarre than the first. Become your spirit—embrace it, project all good things to the cosmos, and the cosmos will reciprocate in kind.

I discovered also, that people become more entertaining in my learning about their sojourns expands my perception of the cosmos. It adds to both theirs and mine, synergistically. Talk to them. Learn what they know and know what they learn. Share your sojourns and learn about theirs. If we forgo the learning of even one person's perceptions of their cosmos, we have lost an infinite number of perceptions. You may have some perceptions in common with them. Others you may not. Transcend our differences by using the formula in this book to negotiate common ground and work to make the Perception Value a positive number, because positive equals truth, which equals trust.

Finally, for inspiration, go to Boothbay Harbor, Maine in September and eat lunch in one of the restaurants overlooking the bay. Bring a pad and pencil, a laptop, whatever you have, and just let your mind go; allow your mind to become the rhythm of the bobbing boats among the seagulls around the incoming tide. And, by all means, let the salt smell of the briny water flow into you, and through your veins, as often as possible, and go on journeys where only the vast open sea is in ahead of you.

Of All Things, Great and Small